SKULL NUGGETS

AMY M. VAUGHN

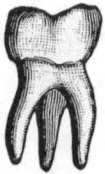

Bizarro Pulp Press
an imprint of JournalStone Publishing

This is a work of fiction. All of the characters, names, incidents, organizations, and dialogue in this novel are either the products of the author's imagination or are used fictitiously.

Bizarro Pulp Press books may be ordered through booksellers or by contacting:

Bizarro Pulp Press, a JournalStone imprint
  www.BizarroPulpPress.com

  ISBN: 978-1-947654-75-4

Printed in the United States of America
JournalStone rev. date: July 25, 2018

  Cover Art: Betty Rocksteady

  Interior Formatting: Lori Michelle
    www.theauthorsalley.com

For Ben

1
READY READY READY

"**H**ELLO JONATHAN.**" Arianne looked past his leopard-spotted hair, past his tattooed face, past the spikey dermal implants lining his jaw, past his doofy, excited grin. She saw past all of it into the future he meant to her. Jonathan was crucial. This conversation was crucial. If she wanted to build her empire, to bring peace of mind to millions, to be the first in the most important line of saviors of the human race, she needed to play this right. She took a deep breath in, and as she exhaled she smiled gently and became visibly more relaxed.

"You ready?" she asked.

"Are you kidding? I'm fucking stoked. Ready ready ready ready ready!"

She knew this. He'd worked hard, spending every possible minute training on the biofeedback machines. He'd struggled with lucid dreaming and ended up needing to sleep with the REM-signaling light mask. But now he was ready. Just in time.

"All right, let's go."

Arianne walked Jonathan into the operating room. His face lit up when he saw the tray of instruments. "Psht. We won't be needing this," he said, pointing to the hypodermic needle for the local anesthetic. Passing over the scalpel and tongs, his hand hovered above the drill for just a second before he could no longer contain himself. He picked it up.

"Oh my fucking God! This is it! This is the fancy-pants drill I couldn't afford!"

Arianne knew she was lucky. If Jonathan had been able to get his hands on a drill like that on his own, he never would have shown up on her doorstep.

"Here," she said, "watch this." She put on thin blue latex gloves and took the drill from him. Pointing it into the air, she turned it on. Its crown-shaped bit whirred to life. She lined it up with the palm of her hand and showed him how the drill would immediately shut off if it ran into anything soft, like flesh or brain.

"So cool," he said.

Jonathan hopped into the dentist chair, and as Arianne eased it back until he was fully reclined, she said, "Sorry about the plastic. I know it's cold, but the procedure does tend to get messy." She knew he didn't care how messy it got. Not only was he going to be free from his consuming angst, he would experience a level of consciousness unknown to most people. To him, it couldn't have been more appealing.

"Ah, here's Doctor David now," Arianne said as a pale, bird-like man entered the room. All but his watery blue eyes were hidden behind the steel-gray surgeon's cap and white face mask. The doctor held his well-scrubbed, gloved hands out in front of him, as if he were holding an invisible newborn baby.

"Ready?" he asked.

"I just need to numb the area," Arianne answered, securing Jonathan to the table. As she strapped his right wrist, she found herself sneaking glances at his mangled hand. Embarrassed, she very purposefully didn't look at it again.

The straps were necessary. He would be awake the whole time, and it wasn't unknown for people to flinch away from the drill or go into uncontrollable spasms during the operation.

"I have to use the lidocaine to make the testing conditions uniform," Arianne told Jonathan as she injected the anesthetic into the center of his forehead.

He didn't want it, but submitted. "You're the boss."

"There," she said, pulling the needle out. "It'll just take a minute to work its way around."

Arianne turned to the doctor. "Have you had a chance to check on the guests in the South Wing?"

"Not yet. I'm headed there after this."

Arianne nodded.

"It's Jonathan, right?" Doctor David asked his new patient.

"Johnnie."

"Ok, Johnnie," said the doctor, poking his index finger around Jonathan's forehead. "Are you ready?"

"Yes sir, yes sir."

"You will be able to feel what we do. It should be pressure but not pain."

"Can you put it in the middle of the tattoo?" Jonathan asked. The chin strap held his jaw in place, so he had to speak from between his teeth.

Doctor David looked at Arianne. "Sure," she said.

With a practiced flick of his wrist, he used the scalpel to trace a nearly perfect circle in the skin of Jonathan's forehead. Arianne sponged up the copious bleeding.

The doctor then used the scalpel to scrape away the circle of skin, revealing a six-millimeter patch of the skull's frontal bone. He lifted the electric drill, pulling the trigger to give it a quick test while it was still in midair. There was a three-second *whirr*. He then centered the drill on the exposed bone and pulled the trigger again. The *whirr* was lower pitched and slower, but not longer.

They were through the first layer of the skull, into the marrow. Arianne knew that Jonathan would be feeling some bubbling and hearing a slurping sound inside his head.

Doctor David pulled the trigger again, giving the drill just the slightest pressure. There was another brief *whirr* and the drill shut off. He was through, and she knew Jonathan was feeling a rush, a lightness, and soon would feel euphoria.

"Tunnel," the doctor said, holding out his hand. Arianne placed the titanium tunnel with its mesh center in his palm. He affixed it to the inside edge of Jonathan's trepanation. It wasn't a worry that the bone would grow back, but the skin was a different matter.

"All done," said Doctor David. "Good job, Johnnie. Easy peasy." And with that, and an off-hand "I'll check in with you before I leave" to Arianne, the doctor peeled off his gloves, threw them in the trash, and was out the door. The whole procedure took fewer than fifteen minutes and left Jonathan with a hole in the center of his forehead, right through the pupil of his third-eye tattoo.

LEAVING THE PSYCH WARD 2

ROBERT PLUNKED HIS ass down on the sun-faded upholstery of the shuttle van and sighed along with his seat cushion. Two weeks on the psych ward and what did he have to show for it, except that his shit was still black from drinking charcoal? He was even being sent home with the exact same medications he'd overdosed on. In fact, even more of them. Score zero for modern psychiatry.

Robert tried to fathom it the whole ride back to the shithole town where his shithole apartment awaited in all its shithole glory. He understood the system, why things happened the way they did, better than most. There was really no one to blame.

He knew, because of his mandatory college internship, that the first seventy-two hours after a failed suicide were the most vulnerable, so that's how long they kept him under close observation. It wasn't anybody's fault that his particular non-lethal cocktail meant he would sleep through those first three days. It wasn't anybody's fault that he woke up to the heartbreak of being alive on the ward. Completely unlike the for-profit facility where he'd done his unpaid servitude, the ward was the only part of the public hospital that hadn't seen a single upgrade since the '80s. It wasn't anybody's fault that the ward's gray tile floors and pistachio green walls were the backdrop to the tremors and spasms that shattered through him while his body processed the chemical overload.

It was nobody's fault that when he could finally function, he had to choose between the isolation of his room or the suspect comradery of the "day room," with its brown vinyl couches and blue plastic chairs. Nobody's fault, not their own or anybody else's, that the day room occupants were each in the throes of their own unique meltdowns and therefore were about as predictable as Schrödinger's cat on bath salts.

None of it was anybody's fault. It's just the way things were.

The desert rolled by. All the scrubby mesquite, pokey ocotillo, and destined-to-be tumbleweeds blending together. From a distance it looked like worn-out Velcro.

The other passengers, all two of them, looked up from their phones when Robert let out a fly that had been banging against his window. He didn't recognize the other men from the hospital. They couldn't have been failed suicides like him, he thought. They looked like real "guys' guys," like the gunshot or hanging type, both methods far more likely to get the job done.

Robert didn't have his phone, which was just as well. There was no one to talk to, no one to text, to tell he was out and headed home. Instead he continued to gaze unfocused out the window and to rehash, to ruminate, as the doctors would say.

Another person not to blame: Dr. Green, the staff psychiatrist. Robert had never seen a more haggard-looking person in his life, at least nobody sober. Green came off as one of those all right guys in an impossible situation—overworked, understaffed, overwhelmed.

From the first time Robert saw him, he felt bad for Dr. Green. There were all the usual signs that the balance of power was tipped heavily to the doctor's side. Green was behind the massive wooden desk and Robert was in the chair without arms. Green was in his suit and tie and Robert was in the hospital-issued scrub pants and white t-shirt. Green had shoelaces and a belt, two things Robert couldn't be trusted with. But Robert's inclination was to make things as easy on Green as he could, to help him out, like he was in a worse place than Robert was.

And if Green's demeanor wasn't enough to signal defeat, his monotonous voice hammered home the resignation.

Green scanned the top few pages of Robert's chart. "Have you heard of neurophages?"

Robert did his best not to visibly shudder. He had to know the question would come. "Only what I've seen on the news."

As if Robert was going to tell him, the guy who could let him out, how much he thought about neurophages. First of all, everyone had heard of neurophages, but most people called them brain mites. Second of all, Robert was completely obsessed with them. Since their discovery nineteen months before, he had read every study, every article, every opinion piece and crackpot conspiracy theory out there. Finally, all that research training as a psych major was proving useful. Not only had he found every scrap of information, but he'd read it all so many times that he knew when a journalist hadn't done their homework. He knew which sources different scientists were predicating their hypotheses on.

Robert thought about brain mites all the time. Even though he knew they were nanoscopic, hardly bigger than a virus, in his mind they looked like tardigrades, commonly known as water bears. He used to think nothing in the world was creepier than water bears, those microbes that look like a cross between an insect and a sleeping bag, with their fat legs with claws on the end. Tardigrades are indestructible. They can be starved, irradiated, sent into orbit— they're fine. They can survive temperatures from 300 degrees to -300 degrees. They're in the ocean, the rain forest, on mountain tops. They've even been found in Antarctica.

Robert's imagination plugged these disgusting little things in as brain mites. He saw them climbing his neurons like vines, making their way to the end of an axon, to the terminal where they latched on with their sarlacc mouths and sucked and sucked, nursing away on his thoughts and memories and dreams.

He thought about brain mites so much that nearly everything he did all day, every day, before failing to kill himself was done in order to not think about them. But every night, the time would come when he couldn't keep reading, or computing statistics, or following guided visualizations, or any of the hundreds of other things he tried to do to keep them away. The time would come when he would be too tired to focus, and there they'd be. Lined up single file, like homeless folks at a soup kitchen, like rich kids for the newest iPhone. Like ants. Or they'd be floating from one neuron to another, copulating, reproducing, multiplying, until there was no more room, until his skull was full to bursting with roly poly brain mites.

Yes, he'd heard of neurophages. As far as he knew, there was no treatment for them. Nobody saw a need. There was some sketchy evidence that people who did a shitload of hallucinogens had fewer of them, but this was interpreted as a neutral finding, or even as evidence against hallucinogens, as if they were messing up some precarious balance.

"Well, then you know that neurophages are tiny organisms that live in our brains and metabolize neurotransmitters," Dr. Green said.

Metabolize!? Robert held it in. How about feed on, eat, steal? How about they are eating my brain right now, as you sit there calmly explaining them to me? How about this conversation is feeding the cycle where I think about them, giving them thoughts about themselves to eat, which makes me think about how they are actually made of thoughts about themselves, so they get more to eat? How about this crazy-making closed loop is what got me in here in the first place?

Dr. Green continued, uninterrupted, "Now, we don't know very much about neurophages yet. We don't even know if they are symbiotic or parasitic little guys."

Little guys! Like they're preschoolers or Pekingese.

"And we don't know their relationship to mental illness. But the best bet is that we evolved with them, like our gut bacteria. So far, we don't know exactly what in the brain they're attracted to. They seem to be indiscriminate feeders. That means serotonin is one of the things they eat. And, as you know, that's the neurotransmitter targeted by most medications prescribed for depression. One thing we do know is that in about ten percent of people who take the medication you're on, the neurophages steadily increase, which in turn lowers the amount of available serotonin. That's why I'm going to recommend an increase in your dosage."

Robert did not take this as good news, to put it mildly. Instead of ending the hideous, slow coup the neurophages were waging on his brain, overdosing had given them an all-you-can-eat buffet. They had been feasting for days, were probably still gorging themselves. And now he was supposed to take *more* medication? Pour more food into their fish bowl? Kick. Ass.

But he said nothing about any of that. Dr. Green was the gatekeeper. The sooner he could convince Green that his little suicidal episode was over, the sooner he could get out of there and find a more effective means of ending his life.

What Robert did say was, "Is there a test to see if I'm in that ten percent?" Some solid data refuting his nightly terrors might go a long way.

"Not one that most insurance . . ." Green looked at the front page of the chart in his hand. "No. No, I'm afraid not. Don't worry," he went on, having no idea what he was talking about, "the increased dosage is our best bet."

✱✱✱

Robert only saw Dr. Green a few more times during his stay. The second time, Green asked things like, "What made you want to kill yourself?" and "What coping strategies have you tried?"

Robert had been in and out of shrinks' offices since he was nine years old. He knew that what you don't say is far more important than what you do. What he didn't say was that he didn't cope. He didn't follow a "healthy schedule." He didn't go for walks in the sunshine, eat fresh vegetables, seek out meaningful interactions. He didn't do any of it. He wallowed. Depression was his mud bath and he was a pig for it, most comfortable submerged in its gritty ooze.

He'd lost every job he'd ever had because of it, was on social security because of it. Because some days, most days, other people were impossible. How could they not see the bizarre uselessness of everything? How could they keep up the charade that any of it matters?

No, Robert would rather just stay home, in his shithole apartment, and wallow.

There had been a reprieve, a girl. But it ended and he was in a worse place than before.

Katherine. If Katherine killed herself, she'd slice her arms open and get blood everywhere, maybe paint with it. One final spectacle on her way out. Something she'd read about in *Juxtapoz*. The week after she left, they discovered brain mites. It was all over the news.

In their next session Dr. Green asked what kind of support structure he'd be going back to. Robert told him he had a friend he checked in with every day. He did not. The person Robert had in mind was the cashier at the convenience store across from his apartment building. A middle-aged guy named Jeff. He was the only person Robert saw every day, except Jeff's days off. They did not talk.

Robert was convinced that it was better not to have people in his life. People are easily breakable. The fewer people in your life, the fewer you have to watch break.

He learned this in grade school, when his broken mother killed herself. And with his grandmother, his dad's mom, who helped raise him. She was always slightly cracked. Nothing major, just endearing little eccentricities. She washed meat with soap before she cooked it. She talked to beams of sunlight. But she was kind, always made a casserole for people in tragedy. And when she broke, passing away peacefully in her grandma bed, under her grandma quilt, Robert's father broke then too—except he kept on living.

Dr. Green would break someday. If Green were to kill himself, he'd probably take pills, hoping it would all just quietly slip away. But he'd back it up by sitting in his running car in his closed garage— a backup plan available only to the relatively well off. If Robert wasn't so poor, he'd have had more options. He wouldn't be a guy who failed to kill himself with pills, probably the most chickenshit of methods.

The last time Robert saw Dr. Green, Green was signing his release papers. Offhandedly he asked, "It says here you live out in Portal. Isn't that where the Forato House is?"

Robert nodded.

"Unorthodox stuff they're doing there, but I guess it's helped some people. Have you looked into it?"

"No," he said, "I haven't."

"Well, maybe you should. Couldn't hurt."

Dr. Green scribbled his signature. "Here you go," he said. "Good luck," and he handed Robert a piece of paper that said he was sane enough to look after himself.

3
MOUNT KAILASH

ARIANNE ABIDED IN the serene clarity that came from sitting next to Lord Shiva. Unaffected by the snow and wind on the Himalayan peak, she settled into the experience of union, no longer a separate self but now an indistinguishable part of the whole.

The first time Arianne had been to Mount Kailash, she'd been overwhelmed, decimated by the power of Shiva's presence. Her spontaneous reaction had been to regress, reverting back through her twenty-eight years, through the desolation of young adulthood, the insecurity of adolescence, the unpredictability of childhood, all the way back to the blind trust of infancy. And in that state of complete vulnerability and dependence, Shiva had gathered her into his arms and held her.

It was the first time she had ever been completely at peace.

The next time she visited, she sat at a distance, where it was somehow easier to maintain the integrity of her being. Any closer and she felt she might vibrate apart, her molecules dissipating out across the universe.

Slowly, over many years, she learned to tolerate the onslaught of the staggering field he projected. The key was to surrender. Gradually, she could move closer to him without regressing. Gradually, she could bring her full self into his presence.

He never spoke. There was no need.

Eventually Arianne realized that the end of this process, of moving ever closer to the font of power, would result in her sitting where he sat, becoming the source. After twelve years of patient progress, the day came. She approached him with all the reverence

10

due to the Lord of Destruction, the Lord of Transformation. He looked at her with all three eyes and smiled. It was the open joy of a proud parent.

She felt rather than heard him say, "Sit into me." She turned her back to him and sat down toward his tiger-skin blanket, expecting to end up on his lotus-folded legs. Instead, she went deeper, easing through him, until she was completely within him, sitting where he sat, as he sat there. Seeing through his eyes. Experiencing his consciousness.

As long as she had taken to become accustomed to his presence, to mature again from infancy to her adult self, nothing could have prepared her for this. The sheer enormity of omniscience kept fear away, along with any distinguishable reaction or sensation at all. Her previous understanding of the world and how it worked was wiped out in an instant, replaced with a wordless explosion of perception, a resolution through immeasurable complexity to a simple, central knowing.

Since that day, she had never needed to join with Shiva again. Instead, it had been enough to simply sit at his left side and settle into the flow of all that is.

Today was no different.

When her time was up, Arianne opened her eyes to the clean room, all white tiles and dentist chairs.

"Charles," she said softly, "I'm back."

A dark-skinned man looked up from his book and smiled, his deep crow's feet stretching back into the curly gray hairs peeking out from under his knit cap. He undid the restraints that held her tight to the chair. "How did it go?"

She told him everything. They were still on track. The boy was coming. His transformation would be magnificent.

HITTING THE ROAD 4

"**W**E'RE GOING TO miss you Bet," the boss man said. She knew he meant it. She was a good employee, a good troupe member, and a great contortionist. "Sexy fire-eaters aren't easy to come by," he said as he leered, lifting an eyebrow and wiggling an imaginary cigar.

"Fuck off, Otis," she said. "You know I'll be back." She'd taken trips like this before, to visit friends on the coast, to backpack national parks, one regrettable time to Burning Man. But she'd always known where she was headed. This time was different. "I just need to find him. Make sure he's ok."

He had hit her up for money, again. This time for rehab. He knew she always had cash. Money was her stepdad's way of keeping her mom from worrying. They'd offered to send her to school, but she'd said not yet, she needed a gap year. That was three years ago now.

With a bio-dad like hers, you didn't get to grow up entirely normal. He hadn't been much of a parent, but he had been a bright, flashing sign that there's more than one way to live a life, that you don't have to play by all the rules.

And now she'd lost him. When she hadn't heard back after sending the money, she assumed that was just him being him. But when she tried to get in touch, when she called the facility, he wasn't there.

"I understand," the carnival manager said, straightening his plaid vest, covering his thick nipple rings. He did that when he was serious. "But remember, door's open. You can come back any time."

Bet stepped out of the camper. Wearing her biggest backpack and her best pair of boots, she set out to find the fuckup who was her father.

5
FORATO HOUSE

WHEN ROBERT GOT back to his small, dark apartment, the only signs he'd been gone were another layer of dust and some rancid orange juice in the fridge. The empty refrigerator reminded him that he'd need to get some food. A jolt of disappointment: he still had to eat. He still had to shit. Still had to shower and brush the teeth of this body he'd tried to discard. What a nuisance. He'd do it later. He opened his laptop and searched on Forato House.

And wow, their website was garbage. It wasn't quite Heaven's Gate bad, but it was like traveling back in time maybe twenty years. The homepage was pale blue with huge text and a thumbnail of the house itself. If Robert hadn't already known what the place looked like, he'd have been at a complete loss. In person, Forato House is big. It's an old, probably historic, Spanish colonial villa that covers at least an acre. The picture, on the other hand, had a strip of brown for the land and blue for the sky with a white rectangle in the middle.

The giant rainbow-colored text said "Forato House" and then something about being "dedicated to the art and science of expanding consciousness to facilitate individual and world peace." Small goals, Robert thought. Under that there were shadowed boxes. One said "Visit," one said "Apply," and the last one said "Project Skylight."

Even though Forato House was only a few miles outside this town where Robert had been living the last few years, it was hardly more than a sign on the road to him. In fact, he'd thought it was a bed and breakfast. He had almost tried to book a room there for a romantic weekend before Katherine left. Katherine, the reason he'd ended up in Portal in the first place.

Robert clicked through the site. Under "Visit" it had a MapQuest still. Under "Apply" it had a list of links labeled "Housekeeping," "Kitchen staff," "Security," and "Test subjects." Each link went to a different application. Test subjects? That was weird.

And then it got weirder.

The graphics on the page under "Project Skylight" had obviously been updated more recently than the rest of the site. Dominating the screen was a picture of a woman's face. She had a hole in her forehead, a hole about the size of a dime. Framing the hole was a tunnel, like the kind people wear in stretched earlobes, and inside the tunnel was white mesh.

A wave of revulsion started in Robert's gut and washed up his throat. Without thinking, he tapped the page closed. He wasn't usually squeamish. He liked to dissect horror movie effects to see how they were done. But seeing that space where skull should be? That was different.

"Damn," he said out loud, startling himself by breaking the silence of the apartment. What the hell was that? Is that what they did at Forato House? Why? He tried to blink the image away, and after a while, it worked.

Late that night, after walking across the street to get his wholesome dinner of a microwave burrito and chips, after sorting out his meds for the week, after reading half a novel and counting a thousand sheep, Robert closed his eyes and immediately felt the brain mites chittering. He could see them, hordes of them now, scuttling around, fighting each other to clasp onto the teats of his neurons. There were more of them than ever, sucking and fucking and expanding. They were filling the space between his brain cells. His gray matter was being squished, flattened under their mass.

The neurophages were destroying the physical substrate of his identity and there was nothing he could do about it. His body reacted with panic. His heart raced, his breath came fast and ragged. He broke out in a full-body sweat. The brain mites, so well fed from his recent colossal fuckup, were squeezing him out of existence. The pressure was insane. Robert held his head in his hands, as if that would keep his skull from bursting, as if anything he did would matter. Any minute now there would be so many of them that they would rupture his eardrums and flow out of his ears. They would ooze out of his eyes, his nose, his mouth, a black and gray and red cascade of brain mites, brain matter, and blood.

And then the image of the hole in that woman's forehead surfaced. It was like that first breath of air after you've been underwater so long you're sure you're going to drown. A hole would let them out. They would spill out like an open tap, gush out like a geyser. All the pressure would be relieved. His brain would have its space back.

Robert opened his eyes, energized for the first time in months. Maybe years. He spent the rest of the night and most of the next morning researching trepanation.

6
RELEASING THE VAPORS OF MANIA AND MELANCHOLY

THE ONLY TIME Robert had heard of trepanation before now was in the first chapter of his Psych 101 textbook, something about ancient cultures making a hole in the skull to release demons or evil spirits. As he read on into the night, it turned out that was pretty much bullshit, not unlike so much else he had accumulated in college along with ever-deferred debt.

His first thought was to go back to the Project Skylight page, but he found he still couldn't stomach the picture and decided to check out more academic sites instead. Trepanation, he learned, is the oldest form of surgery in the world. It isn't brain surgery since it doesn't involve going inside the tough membrane, the dura mater, that protects the brain and spinal cord. It most likely originated with head wounds where bone fragments needed to be removed. Oddness creeps in early though. Archeologists have found hundreds of skulls where there's no evidence of any injury, no clue at all why a hole was made.

All over the world and throughout history, people have used trepanation to treat all sorts of maladies. Specimens have been found from Neolithic Europe and the Inca Empire, to Bronze and Iron Age China, to islands throughout the South Pacific, where they used rocks, shells, and teeth to scrape away bone and expose the underlying meninges. To this day, medicine men in eastern and northern Africa trepan people to treat severe headaches, dizziness, fatigue, epilepsy, and cancer. They use tin can lids and pocket knives.

Hippocrates wrote about trepanation in the 4th century BC. By the 1st century AD, the medical writer Celsus was describing the crown trepan, which looks like a wine bottle opener, only instead of a corkscrew it has a sharpened little crown-shaped device for a tip.

In the 2nd century AD, Galen experimented on the skulls of monkeys and oxen. Because of his studies, and his access to gladiators and their head injuries, he had better success than anyone before him with trepanation. Success was relative, though. This was before germ theory. Very few patients survived.

Sometime mid-morning Robert needed to take a break. He ended up getting a couple single-serving boxes of cereal from Jeff at the Crap Stop. Jeff seemed pretty easygoing; still, Robert imagined the ways the clerk might kill himself there in the store: drinking bleach, electrocution, talking shit to a cracked-out kid with a gun during a holdup. When he got home, Robert realized he didn't have any milk, so he ate the cereal dry before falling asleep in his clothes.

When he woke up a few hours later, he wasn't thinking about brain mites. He was wondering about all those skulls with no sign of damage, the ones with no visible reason to have been trepanned. What he found out next only left him with more questions.

Robert discovered that the history of trepanation goes dry between the Greeks and the Middle Ages. Then, in the late 12th century, something new appears. Roger of Parma wrote about using trepanation to release "vapors" that cause mental illness. He said, "For mania or melancholy the skin at the top of the head should be incised in a cruciate fashion and the skull perforated to allow matter to escape," only he said it in Latin. The operation was referred to as "removing the stone of folly."

Search as he might, Robert couldn't uncover how this use originated, but there's evidence it went on for hundreds of years despite the hazards. And there were, and still are, hazards aplenty: meningitis, encephalitis, tetanus, and brain abscesses for starters. Or cerebrospinal fluid can collect subdurally, putting pressure on the brain, or it can rupture the dura mater and create a leak. The brain can even herniate through the hole. In medieval days, far more people died from the procedure than were ever cured by it, but it must have worked enough of the time to keep doing it.

In 1652, five hundred years after Roger of Parma wrote about "vapors," a scholar named Robert Burton wrote a book called *The Anatomy of Melancholy*. How goth, Robert thought. In this book Burton says "Tis not amiss to bore the skull with an instrument, to let out the fuliginous vapors . . . Guinerius cured a nobleman in Savoy by drilling alone, leaving the hole open a month together by means of which, after two year's melancholy and madness, he was delivered."

Eventually, in Western medicine, lobotomies replaced trepanations. But the lobotomy was fundamentally different. The nature of the lobotomy was to damage, to cut through the frontal lobe. The fallout was that you were, well, lobotomized. Trepanation, when it worked and didn't kill you, left you whole, unbroken.

Robert had a new obsession to go along with his brain mites. Did it work? Was trepanation really a cure for depression? Just because it was old and bizarre, that didn't automatically make it wrong. It could have been like leeches, or like maggots, or like any of those old practices that seem ridiculous and gross but actually have a legitimate place in medicine. There had to be some reason people had been boring holes in their heads for the last twelve thousand years.

Given the opportunity, Robert decided he'd rather drill a little hole in his skull than blow a great big hole clear through it. It just made sense to at least start with the smaller of the two. If that didn't work, he could always trade up.

And either one of those options were better than slogging through life dealing with his depression, with the emptiness, the increased gravity, the aches, numbness, and frustration. The sense that something has to give and at the same time knowing that nothing's going to change.

Desperate times, as the saying goes.

With all this new information, something inside Robert shifted.

He started to sit up a little taller, breathe a little deeper. Was this hope? As he continued to investigate, another undeniable feeling cropped up, again. Hunger. Bodies, always demanding something. So he pulled on his shoes and headed to the communal pantry across the street.

Standing in line with his banana and reheated chili verde dog (it was the only thing left on the rolling grill), he was intrigued by how bright the place looked. The reds and yellows of the junk food packaging seemed shinier. Maybe it was the little spark of optimism. Maybe he was just giddy from walking upright for the first time in months instead of slouched in on himself. Whatever it was, in a moment he was going to act out of character. Everything in his life was about to change on a dime.

7
CRAP STOP ENCOUNTER

BET BROUGHT HER reheated eggrolls and bottled smoothie up to the counter. While the middle-aged cashier rang her up, she asked, "Know anything about Forato House?"

"Not really," he replied.

"I do," said the guy in line behind her.

"Yeah? Right on," she tossed back over her shoulder. She finished paying and stepped aside so he could put his stuff down. She tried to look at him, but he was looking anywhere but at her. Finally, he gave her face a glance and she realized he was not on drugs, as she originally suspected. He was just painfully shy.

"What can you tell me about it?" she asked.

"Well, they aren't a bed and breakfast." He smiled at this, but when he saw Bet's puzzled look, his face went flat. "Sorry, inside joke." She waited while he fished in his pocket for crumpled dollar bills.

"Really I don't know much more than what I've read online," he said, getting his change and stepping away from the counter. They went outside.

"Anything you could tell me, anything at all, I'd really appreciate. I'm looking for my dad. I think he's there."

They ate their sodium bomb dinners sitting against the side of the store and talked about what they'd both read on the website. Robert, because it was, of course, Robert she was talking to, told her where it was relative to the convenience store and that the building was far bigger than it looked in the picture.

She told him about her dad being an irresponsible ass who did a lot of drugs and called himself a seeker and a freak. She talked about how he'd been in and out of trouble her whole life, about how she was trying to track him down and how she'd learned through a friend of his that he was obsessed with Forato House.

Bet noticed she was doing most of the talking. Whenever she paused, Robert would ask her a question. She figured this was as much so he didn't have to talk as for any other reason.

"So, you saw the Project Skylight stuff?" he asked.

"Yeah. I really don't want to believe he's involved with that, but if anyone would let somebody pop a hole in their brainpan, it'd be my dad."

She didn't learn anything new from Robert, but she had a good feeling about him. She liked him. He was tall and lanky, all elbows and knees. He seemed kind and smart—a little self-deprecating— but kind and smart.

The sun had been down for a while and their food was long gone. It was time to go.

"Well, nice to meet you Robert," she said.

"I wish you good fortune in your quest," Robert said, quickly followed by, "Wow, that was just dumb. Sorry."

"Hey," she said, gliding over his discomfort, "you don't know of anywhere I could crash, do you? This place isn't very traveler friendly."

"There's a motel up the road, but it's kind of a dump. You can stay with me if you want. Call it couch surfing." Robert's voice got faster, more nervous, "I mean, that is, if you don't think it's too sketchy to stay with a guy you just met at a convenience store. Never mind. That's ridiculous. My apartment's a studio. It's kind of a mess. You can find a better place. I don't know why I said that."

"I doubt you'll try anything," she said. "And anyway, I'm pretty sure I could kick your ass." She totally could. It was obvious.

8
Brain Blood Volume

ROBERT AND BET talked long into the night. For a while they talked about movies. It turned out they both had a fondness for low-budget horror and a disdain for zombies. They talked about Roger Corman and Lloyd Kaufman. They shared an unexpected love of *Rubber* and a few other absurdly surreal movies, but they disagreed on *Eraserhead*.

"It's just dumb," she said.

"It was groundbreaking."

"A thing can be groundbreaking and still be bad. Like Lovecraft."

He was starting to like her, a lot.

This was the first time in over a year that a female had been in Robert's apartment. The first time since Katherine had picked up the last of her stuff. It was hard for him not to compare the two of them. Katherine had been the sexy librarian he'd dreamed about in high school. Glasses and bangs, pencil skirts and heels. She was serious and coy. The word best fitting Bet was *real*. Bet was genuine. She had a snarky streak and wasn't afraid to tell you how she felt. Katherine did things, acted the way she did, because of articles she read in magazines and on blogs. Everything about her was about her appearance. Bet was rough around the edges and didn't give a shit if you noticed.

They talked for hours. Bet told him she'd spent the last few years with a traveling carnival, performing as a fire-eating acrobat, and that she was learning sword swallowing. Robert hoped his response of "Wow. That's really fucking cool," didn't expose his intimidation and disappointment with his own life in comparison. She had endless great stories. She had traveled. She had met crazy people, famous people, people who were both, people who were neither but were fascinating nonetheless.

Robert had nothing that interesting, or really interesting at all, to talk about. He never mentioned his depression. In his experience, there was no quicker way to get a person to put up their guard than to say "Yeah, I just got out of the psych ward." Maybe admitting to being a convicted pedophile?

Once or twice, or half a dozen times, he had to keep himself from admiring how her black t-shirt hugged her small breasts. He had to look away from the curve of her waist going into her jeans. It was awful. Here was this smart, fit, cute woman in his apartment, and he was growing increasingly attracted to her. He tried to enjoy the conversation for what it was, not to get his hopes up or spiral off into thoughts about everything he lacked—he had nothing to offer someone like her. No job, no prospects, no future. In every way, he was agonizingly average. Not ugly, but not good looking. Not dumb, but not exceptionally bright. Not humorless, but not really funny. Robert thought if he were a color, it would be beige.

Bet would be all the colors of fire.

Eventually she needed to sleep. The only furniture in the apartment was a double bed, an office chair, and a desk. He said he'd sleep on the floor, but she assured him several times that she didn't want him to, that the bed was big enough for both of them to sleep in without accidentally procreating.

Robert acquiesced but stayed up. Sleep had been hard to come by, and he didn't want to spend the next few hours lying next to her, trying not to move around and wake her up. So she went to sleep and he went back online.

If Bet were to kill herself, it would be taking a bullet for someone else.

Over the last three days, Robert had been released from the hospital; discovered trepanation and gotten his hopes up that it might cure his black and scabby depression; and met a phenomenal woman who was now asleep in his bed. He had let go of trying to keep a handle on anything.

So he read some more. He read about the rebirth of trepanation in the '60s. He read that people thought it was a way to get permanently high, the idea being that the hole released some of the restriction on the volume of blood in the brain, brought it back to like when we're little, before the fontanel closes.

He read people's firsthand accounts: Bart Huges, Joe Mellen, Amanda Fielding. All of them raving about the benefits of drilling a hole in your head. Huges claimed the increased blood volume allowed more parts of the brain to function simultaneously. Mellen wrote a whole book about it. It's called *Bore Hole*.

Robert watched Fielding's self-trepanation, a very bloody film. In it she describes the effect as "a lifting upwards, like the tide coming in, and at the same time a feeling of relaxation and silence in the head, a peace, a stopping of the voice in the head."

That struck Robert hard. Peace? Stopping the voice in the head? What he wouldn't give to have that happen. Whole weeks went by when Robert was so down that all he could think about was how down he was. There were times when he was just there, sitting on the toilet with his elbows on his knees, his head in his hands, his stinking shit in the bowl, but he didn't get up because he couldn't find a reason to. Quieting the voice in his head would mean everything, because that voice was telling him it would be easier to just not do this anymore. *This* being any of it. Why get up in the morning? Why eat? Just so you can shit again and go to bed and get up and eat and shit again the next day? Just so you can continue to wear out your clothes and your bed and your welcome everywhere you've ever gone? It would be better for everyone involved if he just wasn't there. One fewer person on his therapist's clock. One fewer person taking up space and air and water.

If he could get that voice to shut up, he thought, that'd be worth drilling a hole in his head.

All told, maybe two dozen people trepanned themselves as part of this '60s mini-movement, including at least one American, Peter Halvorson, but he'd have to wait. Robert needed sleep, although he almost couldn't because he was too excited about what he'd found. Eventually, though, he became too tired to ward off the brain mites. They came, they squirmed, they danced. Finally, in his anxious delirium, Robert found himself counting giant tardigrades as they jumped over a little white fence. Bo Peep looked on, horrified.

9
FINGERBANG AND THE SKINHEADS

JOHNNIE WAS ON stage with his band Fingerbang. They were playing at an old warehouse in the industrial part of town. The acoustics were crap but nobody cared. Johnnie knew he was probably tone deaf, but they always drew a crowd. People showed up because of the one thing you could count on at every Fingerbang show: Johnnie would bleed. Every show, one way or another.

Afterward people would come up and ask, "How do you do it? How do you make it look so real?"

When he told them it *was* real, that he did it by actually doing it, by cutting himself, most of the time the conversation ended right there. Give people the illusion of pain and they're happy; real pain gives them the heebie jeebies, freaks them out. But there were some, just a few, who would ask "What's it like?" or "Have you ever had to get stitches?" or "Why? Isn't life painful enough?"

It was hard to explain why. It wasn't that he hated himself. It wasn't, like some cutters say, because he wanted to feel something.

Sometimes he thought it was for the moment of reprieve. The moment when the world went away and his mind was completely overtaken with the sensation of the slice. The moment before the pain, when you know the pain is coming. And then the burning white sting of the air as it touches red flesh.

Sometimes he thought it might be for the Russian roulette with cutting too deep or in the wrong place, or with infection. Johnnie wasn't trying to be GG Allin or even Sid. He usually used a straight razor, which he kept very sharp and very clean, but still, the clubs they played were grimy places. Sepsis loomed.

Sometimes he thought it was for the necessary reminder that he was an animal made out of meat. See, there it is. People forget that they are no more, no less than meat walking around, like a deer or a cow. Bodies are fragile, pain comes easy. Carpe diem and all that shit.

Always though, he cut himself because other people, normal people, didn't. Because they thought it was crazy—maybe stupid, maybe repulsive—but it was something they would never do. It was his thing. Since the accident, since getting his hand split in two, his body had been a permanent transgression. It made him as much a freak on the outside as the inside, and he ran with it. Tattooed, pierced, implanted, cut, branded, bleached, and dyed.

He'd tell people he was a walking artistic statement, that he was trying to wake people up out of their stupor. He said pain brought him clarity. It was a spiritual practice because it wouldn't let you leave the present moment no matter how much you tried to escape. Most of that was bullshit, but he really wanted it to be true.

Fingerbang tore into their anthem, "Pity Sex." Johnnie was screwing up the lyrics. He just kept repeating "If I bled for you, would you fuck me then?" Nobody cared or even noticed. This was normal. Lyrics were not why people showed up. He was trying though, trying to think of the other words, the refrain, anything, but he kept getting distracted by skinheads. He noticed maybe five of them spread throughout the bobbing and weaving crowd.

Maybe they'll stay cool, he thought, and not start any shit. But he knew that was a long shot.

By the time the song was winding up, after a whole minute and forty-five seconds, Johnnie had spotted three more, four more. Then the song was over. People cheered. When the cavernous warehouse grew quiet, he could hear the pops, like gum bubbles bursting, as people—pop—turned into skinheads. It only took a minute and everyone in the crowd had turned into a skinhead. Pop, pop, pop, bald heads and Doc Martens.

Oh shit, I'm dreaming, Johnnie thought. But then he

remembered. No, I'm tripping, strapped to a chair in a research facility on the Mexican border.

As the band started another song, the faces of the skinheads changed. Their eyes grew huge, bulged out from their sockets, and became segmented, like bees' or flies' eyes. Johnnie watched, fascinated, while he sang the lyrics he could remember for "Clown Whore." The skinheads' noses and mouths grew into tubes, like hoses stuck onto their faces with puckering sphincters at the end.

Oh right, he thought, brain mites. I'm supposed to battle these fuckers.

The skinheads kept becoming more insect-like. Here and there, Johnnie watched as a body swelled out into maggot shape, its cuffed blue jeans, white polo, and skinny suspenders becoming part of its huge, slimy body.

Ok, I've trained for this, he told himself. I'm in control. I can make anything happen here.

Johnnie dropped his mike and grabbed his straight razor. Blocking out everything else, he willed the blade into a giant sword. He touched it and blood appeared on his finger, but he didn't feel anything. That shit was sharp as hell.

"Let's go motherfuckers!" Johnnie hollered as he leapt from the two-foot-high stage and started wailing on the man-sized, pulpy white maggots. Sweeping in smooth arcs from side to side, the sword went through the giant bugs effortlessly, slicing them open so their mushy gray guts could spill out. By the time he got through the first couple rows, everyone in the warehouse had been maggotized. They wobbled and slithered, all of them moving in his direction.

Johnnie felt panic start to take over. There were dozens of these fuckers. Even if they weren't armed—literally, he thought, by now most of them had no arms—there were so many of them. As they closed in on him, he pictured himself suffocating under a pile of giant skinhead maggots.

But he held onto the idea that this was his hallucination. What would be the ultimate weapon against these assholes? He needed something lighter, something faster. He concentrated and turned his sword into a light saber. When he saw that it was pink and strobing, he was a little disappointed. But he chalked it up to the blinking pink light of the lucid dream training mask he'd had to wear during his preparation. Dealing with it, he took his flashing pink light saber and went to town. Bvrumm, bvrumm, bvrummmmmm. He slashed down wave after wave. Skinhead maggot innards piled up around him. He had to slosh through the funky guts to find a clear patch and regain his footing, slicing and dicing as he went.

Finally, only three were left. They closed in on him, two from the front and one from behind him. "You'll never be rid of us," one of the sacs in front of him said, its fly anatomy turning the words into kazoo sounds.

He knew it was right, but it didn't matter. "We'll never be rid of cockroaches," he said, "but that doesn't mean you don't kill the disgusting fuckers when they move into your house. And this is most definitely my house, and you are most definitely disgusting fuckers."

He gave the last three skinhead maggots extra slicing up, until they were noodles on the floor. He only had a moment to appreciate his handiwork, a warehouse flooded with bug guts, before, in the outside world, he blinked. He was coming out of it.

Johnnie woke up strapped to the chair. Arianne was there.

"How did it go?" she asked.

"That was awesome! When can I go again?"

10
PROJECT SKYLIGHT

THE NEXT MORNING, before Robert opened his eyes, his first thought was, as always, about brain mites—a flash of them scurrying around, eating their fill, replicating themselves. His second thought was about the hole and the bugs pouring out of it. Then he remembered Bet. And, finally, he realized that for the first time since he'd started medication, he had morning wood.

His eyes shot open. From the look of things, Bet had been up for a while. She was sitting at the desk, swiping through something on her phone.

"Good morning," she said.

"Goo-ack." He coughed, turned red with embarrassment, and tried again. "Good morning."

"I've been looking over the Forato House site again. It's terrible. Heaven's Gate should be jealous."

"I completely agree. Did you find a phone number?"

"I called when I first heard of the place. They said they couldn't tell me if he was there because it would violate their privacy policy. I just need to find a way in, so I can see what's going on, see if he's in there doing something dumb."

She looked back down at the little screen and Robert seized the opportunity.

"I'm just going to take a quick shower," he said too fast, and he made an awkward dash to the bathroom.

After taking care of the things that needed taking care of, Robert asked Bet if she'd like to get something to eat, his treat. He didn't have any money but he had a credit card, and the future in which he'd have to repay the debt was completely unreal to him. He was leaning in hard to the idea of Project Skylight. Somewhere along the way, he had formed the notion that it would be his rebirth, erasing everything that had come before.

For the first time maybe ever, Robert felt carefree.

He chose to take Bet to the better of the two cafés on the main drag. Really both were average and both had their specialties. This one had local, organic produce and the other one had a well-seasoned fryer.

Bet waited until their food was served to start the real conversation. She ordered a burger and fries, of course.

"Do you think my dad is really doing that Project Skylight thing? It's pretty drastic."

"I don't know," Robert hedged. "I guess I can understand how somebody might see it as a viable option."

"Man, you'd have to be hella desperate."

Robert shrugged noncommittally. "Was he?"

"Was he desperate? I don't know. I only know what he told me, which I'm pretty sure was a bald-faced lie. He said he needed help getting off opiates. That was an easy sell. I could totally see him developing a heroin problem. As much as he claims to be looking for answers to the big questions of life, I think he'd be happy to settle for the questions just going away."

She took another bite. "These fries are kinda lame," she said, killing him a little. New method of suicide: letting Bet down. "Anyway, I applied for a job there online this morning, housekeeping."

"Do you think they'll notice that you're his daughter?"

"Nah," she said. "We have different last names since he legally changed his to Curseword."

They were back in the apartment. Bet was on her phone. Robert assumed she was checking in with friends because that's what other people did on their phones. So he hunkered down over his laptop, making sure she couldn't see the screen. After what she'd said about it at the café, he didn't want her to know he was seriously considering Project Skylight. Maybe it was crazy, but what he read next, about Peter Halvorson, sold him past the close.

Halvorson found trepanation in his search to cure his intractable depression. This was the first modern account Robert had come across of using trepanation to cure mental illness. Halvorson drilled a hole in his skull just above his forehead in 1972. In his description of it he said, "I was almost instantly free of my interpreting neurosis. The 'question and answer' game in my head, that never got resolved, simply disappeared."

Decades later, Halvorson started a trepanation advocacy group, but doctors in the U.S. wouldn't touch it with a ten-foot drill bit. So he started leading small groups to be trepanned by neurosurgeons south of the border. All of the participants in his medical tourism jaunts had to agree to a battery of studies, including brain imaging.

And so it was that Peter Halvorson, some guy from rural Pennsylvania, became the world leader in scientifically documenting the physiological and psychological effects of boring a hole in your skull. He wanted to prove that trepanation did what people who'd done it said it did: cured depression and anxiety; created a sense of calm and well-being; and just generally made your brain work better. But most important to Halvorson was proving the underlying cause of these effects, which, like Huges and Mellen and Fielding, he claimed was increasing the volume of blood in the brain.

Robert tried to find the studies on the medical tourists. From what he could gather, those were the only controlled experiments ever done on elective trepanation. But neither the results nor the original data were published anywhere online.

Maybe it was coincidence, or maybe it was because the study of trepanation was such a limited field, but his searches kept leading him back to the Forato House website. The picture of the woman with a mesh screen implanted in her forehead kept popping up on his screen, the same one he'd found repulsive just a few days before. Now it didn't even faze him. He'd been desensitized. He clicked around the site to see if they had any information on Halvorson's studies.

Scrolling down, he skimmed their brief rendition of the history of trepanation. There was nothing new until the end. Turns out, the first round of Halvorson's studies was declared inconclusive because brain-imaging scans didn't show anything happening. The most recent statement from the advocacy group said they were still holding out for more sensitive imaging techniques, which they were sure would show greater blood volume and increased metabolism throughout the brains of people with nuggets removed from their skulls.

But what had shown up in the meantime, since the end of these studies and the beginning of Project Skylight, was brain mites. What Robert read next would compel him to action.

"At the Forato House, we do not claim that there is any scientific certainty that trepanation, on its own, cures certain mental illnesses or leads to a higher state of consciousness. We agree that there is sufficient anecdotal evidence to warrant further testing. However, our mission is different.

"Beginning with the sparse but statistically significant evidence that people who have regularly taken hallucinogens have fewer neurophages, we have formulated an important hypothesis that we are currently testing in one of our most exciting experiments to date.

"By injecting our proprietary hallucinogenic formula directly into the brain through trepanation holes, and using a process similar to lucid dreaming wherein the underlying mechanisms of the mind are anthropomorphized, we believe we can facilitate the eradication of neurophages and restore positive affect to those who suffer from mood disorders such as anxiety and depression. We are also investigating whether this practice expedites the experience of equilibrium and peace of mind in people with and without a history of mental illness."

Robert couldn't fill out the application fast enough.

When he was done, he checked to make sure there was enough open credit on his card to cover all the fees. At the time, he was too excited to question why they were asking for payment instead of offering it like most trials with human subjects.

All that done, Robert got into bed next to Bet and slept like a kid on cough syrup.

In the morning, he steeled himself and told Bet, "I applied to Project Skylight."

There was a long pause. "Wow," she said. "Thank you."

It wasn't the reaction he expected, which was more along the lines of, "Don't be a fucking idiot," so he just nodded his head a little.

"Really, that might be the most generous thing anyone has ever done for me." She sat next to him on the bed and took his hand. "Look, I promise we won't be there long. We just need to find out if my dad's there and, if he is, convince him to leave. It shouldn't take more than a couple of days."

11
Asking a Favor

ARIANNE WAS PLEASED with herself. She'd received the boy's application that morning. As much as she said none of it was about her—she was just the conduit—she knew deep down it couldn't happen without her.

She wouldn't reply right away. She'd make him wait like any other applicant. The anticipation built up expectations. And the world was nothing if not the manifestation of our own expectations.

But she needed to nip this potential ego trip in the bud. She wasn't going to get carried away, not like her parents. This wasn't a cult. She wasn't going to ride that wave of fervor and fear. She was just offering people the best versions of themselves. Offering freedom from pain, freedom from the past. The opportunity to live forever in the joyful present. No, this was not religion. This was science, with a little help from the Universal Mystery.

She set aside a stack of folders and shut her computer all the way down, password protected. That work could wait. She needed to find Jonathan.

"I need to ask you a favor, Jonathan."

"Sure man, anything. Anything, anything."

She knew that between the trepanation and his first trip, he was riding high. The world was all roses to him right now. He probably really would agree to anything, but her request was simple.

"Pretty soon we're going to get our final recruit for Project

Skylight. I know you signed the non-disclosure agreement. I know I said not to talk about the procedure with anyone behind you in the process, but I want you to talk to this person. Answer anything he asks."

Jonathan was her most ardent convert, or at least her most animated. She knew his enthusiasm would be contagious. And it was important that the new recruit be completely sold. It was the most important thing.

"You got it boss," he said. "No sweat, no sweat."

12
FAMILY SIMULACRUM

IT TOOK ABOUT a week before either of them heard back from Forato House, Bet for her housekeeping position and Robert for his application to Project Skylight. During that time, they did together all those things they would normally have done on their own. Well, the things Robert would normally have done. Bet was from the carnival. Robert had no idea what a normal day was like for her. He imagined it included an outdoor breakfast with all the performers and roustabouts, though he wasn't sure they still used that word anymore. Then securing stuff called "rigging," practicing acts, and generally getting ready for the show.

He and Bet didn't do anything nearly that interesting or productive.

Early in the week they took Bet's orange '80s-era Civic to the grocery store, and after that they just hung out. They read books, made food, and took walks at night, after the beating sun went down.

He grew comfortable around her.

One night they watched *Spider Baby* on Robert's laptop. They were sitting on the apartment floor leaning back against the bare wall. Bet asked, "Want a pillow?" She grabbed the pillows off the bed, and they used them to cushion their backs against the wall. In more than two years of watching videos this way, Robert had never thought to use a pillow. Depression leads to tunnel vision. His had made categories so concrete that it never occurred to him to move things from one zone of the apartment to another. Bed things never left the bed.

He learned a lot about himself being around Bet. Most of the insights were double-edged swords like the pillows. He'd gain some self-awareness that revealed just how utterly fucked he was. But after that he'd begin to see things differently, or at least notice when he was trapped in a ridiculous pattern.

When the movie was over, Bet popped up and said, "Let's go for a walk." She hated being cooped up in the apartment. She was used to being active, what most people would consider strenuously so, and she waited all day for sundown.

So they walked. They walked down the three blocks of the main drag, past the closed strip malls and the bank, the two cafés and the post office. After eight p.m., nothing was open but the Crap Stop.

Bet noticed a strip of dirt separating the Dairy Queen from the barber shop.

"Is that a trail?" she asked.

"It's just a wash," he said, but she was already heading down the embankment. Without Bet, Robert never would have thought to explore a dry wash bed. He probably wouldn't have even seen it. But he followed her, and then he was in it, feeling the loose sand shift under his feet with every step.

"I think there might be snakes around here, maybe coyotes," he warned her. She waited for him to catch up and said, "But it's beautiful."

Once they got away from the street lights, it really was beautiful. The sky was bright enough, with the three-quarter moon, that they could see the jimson weeds spreading and morning glories vining along the banks. The dark shapes of the bigger, scrubbier mesquite and manzanita rose up on either side.

The path was clear and just wide enough for them to walk side by side. Within minutes it felt to Robert as if they were far from town, alone in the desert at night. He didn't know if the crickets were unusually loud or if it just seemed that way because there were no other sounds. Between the stars and the moon and the night-blooming flowers, even he knew this was romantic. If he'd had any balls, he would have taken her hand. But he didn't. He'd never been a first-move kind of guy.

They'd been walking for maybe a mile or two, Robert didn't really know how to judge, when up ahead, the wash changed. They were coming to a culvert, where the floor and the sides of the little ravine were sprayed with cement to keep them from eroding, and a large drainage pipe led under a road. As they got closer, Robert noticed a dark patch against the light-colored concrete. They were nearly on top of it before it took the shape of a person shrouded in a blanket, leaning against a stuffed backpack.

Robert slowed down, thinking this was a very good sign that it was time to turn around and head back. Bet did not slow down. She headed right for him. Or her. Or whoever. Robert grew more uncomfortable. Homeless people made him feel guilty. He had what they didn't have for no other reason than chance. Plus, there was the fact that so many homeless people are crazy. And not like medicated crazy, like the people in the psych ward. Homeless crazy people were not usually able, he assumed, to get the kinds of psychiatric medications best suited to their needs.

But Bet went right up to him. It was a him.

"Beautiful night, isn't it?" she asked.

"It is indeed," he said.

"I'm Bet," she said, offering her hand. She was going to let him touch her.

"I'm Salvio," he said, bringing his hands out from inside his huddle of blankets, but he did not reach for Bet's. Instead, he held up a scruffy strip of fur, barely more than a handful, "and this is Theodore."

"Oh look, Rob, it's a kitten!"

"Wanna hold him?" Salvio asked, looking from Bet to Robert and back to her. Robert knew the homeless man had seen a flash of disgust cross his face. He couldn't help but wonder what kind of diseases the cat was carrying. It almost certainly had worms and thousands of insects in its fur. No, Robert did not want to hold it.

"Oh yes, thank you," Bet said as she took the mewling thing from Salvio's filthy hands. "Do you know how old he is?"

"I do not. I found him a few days ago, just a ways up this wash. I been trying to keep him safe. You know coyotes run through here, and he'd be less than a snack for a coyote."

"That's very kind of you to keep him safe," Bet said while Robert shifted from foot to foot, willing himself not to bolt back down the wash the way they'd come, waiting for their conversation to end, for her to give the cat back so they could leave.

"Yeah," Salvio went on, "but it's no good. I can't feed him right. He needs a home. He probably needs a vet."

"Poor thing," she said. It wasn't clear whether she was talking about the man or the kitten. "What do you think, Rob? Can we help him out?"

"I'm going to be at Forato House if they accept my application," he answered. It was true and noncommittal. He didn't want to tell her no. Ever. He was, after all, a heterosexual man, and what straight guy in his right mind would want to say no to a beautiful, smart, funny, fire-eating, *sword-swallowing acrobat* with whom he was sharing a bed but with whom he had not actually done the deed? So no, he did not say no to the kitten.

"Forato House," Salvio broke in. "Don't go there, son. Something wrong with that place. People don't come back from there."

"He won't be staying long," Bet said to him. Then she said, as if she were talking to the cat, "I'll be at the apartment. Even if I get the job, it'll be shift work. I'll be home at least part of the day. We won't keep Theodore forever." She held the kitten up to her face and rubbed its cheeks with her thumbs, "We'll just get him healthy and then find a family for him. We'll foster him." And for the first time since she'd picked up the mangy thing, she looked at Robert. His discomfort was plain, even in the dim light.

"Oh, but we don't have to. It's your place. It's totally up to you."

But she had called it "home," he thought. "I'll be home part of the day," is what she said.

"We can take him home," Robert said.

Bet snuggled the disgusting kitten all the way back to the apartment complex. As they climbed the stairs, Robert's neighbor walked out onto the landing. The man was morbidly obese with curly dark hair, like Captain Lou Albano but without the rubber bands and much, much bigger. He nodded, and Robert nodded back. That, until then, had been the extent of their interaction whenever they couldn't politely ignore each other. They didn't even know each other's names.

Then the neighbor saw the scruffy thing in Bet's hands.

"Got a kitten, huh?"

"Just fostering, getting it healthy and finding it a home," Robert said quickly. He didn't want Captain Lou to tell the apartment manager, costing him half a month's rent as a pet deposit.

"I had a cat," the neighbor said. "Lived eighteen fucking years. Pissed on every goddamn thing. Just died this last winter."

"Oh, I'm sorry for you loss," Robert said.

"Yeah. Fucking pets. They just die on you."

"Ok, well, you have a good night."

Robert stayed with the cat and Bet drove to the next town over to get essential kitten supplies, like a litter box and food. While she was gone he gave the little thing some milk, although he was sure he'd read somewhere you're never supposed to do that. But Theodore loved it and perked up. The kitten rubbed his grimy face across Robert's shins. He managed to give it a bath in the kitchen sink and dry it off with a hand towel, with only minor blood loss on his part. Then he found a piece of string and tied it around a pencil stub, which he dangled and dragged for the kitten to bat at and chase. When Bet got home, Robert was surprised to find he felt a pang of jealousy when Theodore left him to investigate her.

The rest of the week they settled into a semblance of family life, just the three of them.

13
THE TOUR

"**EVERY ELEMENT OF** Forato House is designed to inspire comfort," Arianne said as she led Robert on the welcome tour. "We want everyone here to be completely at ease."

The building was bigger than most people expected, less of a house and more of a fortress. Sitting at the end of a long dirt road, its imposing dimensions were hard to gauge until you were close. As you walked up to the massive wooden double doors, the impression was that things here were sturdy. The effect continued inside with Saltillo tile, thick wooden furniture, and wrought-iron fixtures. Combined with the subdued lighting, a person couldn't help but feel safe and relaxed. The place was strong, solid, and down to earth.

Off the entryway, they walked through the lounge, which doubled as the building's library. It was lined with books and had an enormous fireplace that went unused except during the few cold weeks when fires were justified this far south. The few people populating the chairs and couches looked up at them and smiled, friendly (like everyone they came across for the rest of the tour). They all wore either hats or bandanas or bangs. None of their foreheads were visible.

Arianne Forato carried her large frame with poise. Her choice to wear brightly colored kaftans and head scarves only increased her formidable presence. The only jewelry she wore was a simple silver chain around her neck with a dime-sized disk on it. The disk had a hole through the center where the chain slid through. If you didn't know better, you'd think it was made of stone. Arianne's eyes gleamed when she smiled and pierced when she didn't. She was never on neutral. She was either taking in or giving out. Right now she was giving out. She was determined to be completely honest with Robert, but she knew subtlety was going to be important. She didn't want to overwhelm him.

"Through here is the dining room. We have a Michelin-star chef who creates the menus. Healthy, beautiful, local cuisine." She watched Robert as she said this, to see if it mattered to him. He simply bobbed his head, the same as he had been doing since he got there. Passive agreement, just receiving information.

They turned right, into the North Wing where the guest rooms were located. Halfway down the hall they passed an alcove that led to the courtyard. Arianne showed Robert his room and gave him his key card. "We're at low occupancy right now, just running the one experiment, so the rooms on either side of you are empty," she said. He left his duffle bag there and they continued on. He still had not said more than "thank you" and "ok." A less confident person than Arianne might have been frustrated by his lack of responsiveness.

The pair continued around the giant square of Forato House. The East Wing looked a lot like the North, except it was shorter and the doors that lined it were irregularly spaced. These were offices and conference rooms. At the end of the hall was a white door with a push bar. Across it were blazoned the words "NO ADMITTANCE WITHOUT ESCORT." It was strikingly different than the wooden doors that lined the hallway.

"Through there is where the magic happens!" she said, and then she opened one of the wooden doors to the left. "This is my office. Let's sit and talk."

Arianne sat down behind her heavy wooden desk. Robert sat in one of the two comfortable armchairs across from her.

"Do you have any questions for me? You can ask me anything." Arianne gave Robert what she hoped was an ingratiating smile.

"How soon can I get trepanned?" Robert asked.

"Soon," she said. "As soon as you finish training."

The muscles around Robert's eyes and mouth flexed, just for a second. Was it just disappointment or was there something else? Hesitancy? Distrust?

"It's not that bad," she went on. "Some people whiz through the preparation in just a few weeks. Being able to control your thoughts and emotions is important, or the experiment can lead to erratic results."

Erratic, that was true enough for now, Arianne thought.

"What's the training entail?"

"You just need to learn to regulate your heart rate and brainwave patterns while you're awake and asleep. Then you'll be good to go." Robert's eyes opened wide and Arianne gave a genuine laugh, revealing deep joy lines around her eyes. "I guess put that way, it sounds pretty intimidating. But we've done everything we can to streamline the process. You'll see. We have the most up-to-date biofeedback equipment and lucid dreaming technology. It will also depend a lot on your previous experience in controlling your attention and how driven you are to move along in the process."

"When can I get started?"

"This afternoon," she answered, looking down at his chart. "Looks like your guide will be Marcus. He's good at his job. Knowledgeable and dependable." Then she added, urged on by his eagerness or maybe her own, "Some people are gifted in navigating their consciousness. If you turn out to be one of them, and I have a feeling you will, I may take you on personally. And, if you want to go further after the initial study, to stick around for Phase Two, you'll be given that option." As she spoke, Arianne took off her head scarf.

Robert eyebrows went up. He sat a little taller, maybe tenser. She couldn't tell if he was surprised or apprehensive.

"I'm sorry," she said putting her scarf back on. "That might have been too much too soon. I didn't mean to make you uncomfortable."

"No. No, it's ok. I just didn't recognize you from the photo on the website until you took your scarf off. A question?"

"You can ask me anything."

"Why would you need a Phase Two if you've gotten rid of all your neurophages?"

"Well," Arianne hesitated, not sure how much to say. She didn't want to scare him away, to add to any wariness he may be feeling, but she didn't want to mislead him either. She took a breath and followed her gut.

"To meet God."

14
MEETING JOHNNIE CURSEWORD

IF **ARIANNE WERE** to kill herself, it would be for a cause. She'd draft a press release for it, keep a webcam on herself as she injected an overdose into her brain portal. Live broadcast her last words.

Robert only had a few minutes before lunch after his tour. This was a good thing. Any longer and he probably would have given in to his chickenshit nature and run. Instead, he went back to his room and unpacked.

On the way to the dining hall, he wondered if he'd be able to recognize Bet's dad. She had said not to worry about it, that he stood out in a crowd. As Robert pushed open the door, he realized he was about to be in a room, on his own, with all of the other participants in Project Skylight. What was he in for? What was he doing here?

There were ten people in the dining room, maybe eleven. Robert was surprised to find that they were normal, just folks. Some old, some not so old. Some a little tan, some darker brown. It looked to be about an even split between male and female. Most had white circular indentations in their foreheads; only one or two didn't. And one guy had leopard-spotted hair and a shitload of face tattoos. That had to be him, Johnnie Curseword.

Robert stumbled through the process of getting his food. Of course, he started at the wrong end of the line, and he asked where the silverware was when it was right in front of him. He even turned around right into a woman, causing her to spill her tray all over herself and the man next to her. But they didn't get mad. Nobody seemed at all put out by his bumbling idiocy. Everyone was friendly.

Finally, he got himself and his tray to Johnnie's table. "Mind if I sit here?"

Johnnie replied by jutting his chin up in assent as he ripped an orange segment from its rind with his teeth.

Everything Robert had scripted and rehearsed, all his plans about being laidback and unaffected when he found him, went out the window. Instead he started in with the old I'm-new-here-and-so-nervous-I-probably-just-wet-myself routine. It came naturally.

"Have you been here long? I just got here. Of course you've been here a while. You already have a hole. Did it hurt? That was a dumb question. I'm sorry. I'm a little anxious about this whole thing. I just got here today. Not knowing anybody sucks. I'm really not the best at social situations, obviously."

He took a breath and looked at Johnnie with a pathetic mixture of chagrin and hopefulness, hoping Johnnie would make it easy for him and spare him from delving further into this awkwardness.

Instead Johnnie said, "No."

"No?" There was an uncomfortably long pause while Johnnie continued chewing. "No what?" Robert asked.

Finally Johnnie swallowed and went on. "No, it didn't hurt. They numb the whole area, so you feel pressure but not pain."

"Oh," Robert said, still not sure what direction this conversation was taking.

"If you want to know what it's like, I can tell you. But most people wouldn't want to hear about it while they're eating."

"Oh! Oh sure, I get it. Surgery is so rarely polite mealtime conversation." Robert smiled, hoping they were sharing a joke. Johnnie just nodded.

They set up a time to meet in the courtyard that afternoon after Robert's first biofeedback session, which meant Robert had plenty of time after lunch to sit in his room and beat himself up about whether or not he should tell Johnnie that he knew Bet. He'd agreed to wait for a sign from her before saying anything, which was fine with him since, if Robert told him, Johnnie might think he was only there with her, and then he might not talk to him about the procedure and the experiment. But, if he didn't tell him and Johnnie found out later, then Johnnie would think he was . . . what? Inconsiderate at the least. Conniving? Deceitful?

He wanted to tell him. He wasn't good at keeping secrets. They made him feel guilty. But what would he say? That she wanted to rescue him? A grown man? That she thought Robert was only here to help her convince Johnnie to leave? That he thought she was amazing and just so together and kind, but not in the pushover way but in the compassionate but realistic way? That he was probably in love with her? That he had come close to telling her how he felt the night before, but didn't want to ruin it? Didn't want her to change how she acted toward him? That she's still living at his place, with their kitten? That she'd be staying there between her housekeeping shifts at Forato House that started today?

There was no clear answer, and all the flawed alternatives played themselves out over and over in his head.

At least he wasn't thinking about brain mites.

15
Bet's First Day

"**I**T'S NOT LIKE a hotel housekeeping job, more like hospital housekeeping," the man in the white scrubs said.

"That's cool. I'm down for whatever. I just really need a job, you know?" Bet replied.

"How do you feel about bedpans?"

"I've never actually used one but I'll try anything once," she joked. He smiled. She went on, "Look, give me gloves and I'll empty whatever you need me to."

"You'll also have to help the nurse change bedding, sometimes with people still in the bed. Most of the time we hire big guys for this type of work. It takes a lot of upper body strength."

"Well, I could show you how many handstand pushups I can do and take this firmly into the category of weirdest first day ever if you'd like."

"No," he said. "Thanks, but that won't be necessary. You're just lucky we need somebody right away. Ok, follow me."

As they walked, he talked about how it wasn't easy to find people this far out in the sticks, how the benefits were good and they'd get to that paperwork later. They went through a cafeteria, and then down a hallway lined with wooden doors. There were a few people around; some of them had silver circles in their foreheads. But none of them were her dad.

"We'll need you to work the swing shift, and you'll have to get some scrubs," he went on. They came to a white door. "You'll get one of these this afternoon," he said, indicating the key card he used to open an electronic lock. They entered a blindingly white hallway.

"It's just down here. You'll be working in the South Wing."

"Do we ever rotate through other positions? Other wings?"

"No, Ms. Forato says predictability is really important for the guests in the South Wing. So the people who work there don't mix much with everybody else. It's not bad though." They arrived at another locked white door. "Most everybody in here is easy to handle, some are even a pleasure to be around. Sounds weird, but it's true."

Bet followed him into the large room. It looked like a hospital ward, with beds lined up on either side. She scanned the faces. Her dad was not there.

This was going to be harder than she thought.

16
BIOFEEDBACK

AT ROBERT'S FIRST biofeedback session, Marcus, who introduced himself as his technician, led him beyond the white door and into the West Wing. Marcus had one of those deep, resounding voices that only huge black guys have, which fit since he was a huge black guy.

Marcus led Robert into a long white room, seriously white. White tile on the floors and on the walls. White panels on the ceiling with white fluorescent lights. White division walls separating six stations. Each station had a different configuration of equipment, most of which was white.

"We'll be in here today," Marcus said, guiding Robert toward the first pod on the left. It had the most equipment. Robert sat in the white chair in the center of the station, and Marcus started hooking him up to the machines—strapping a band around his chest; sticking adhesive electrodes to his hands and arms and chest and head. Wires cascaded off of Robert and into tangled knots that resolved in midair; from there they wound their way into multicolored ports.

"This first session is just to get a baseline. We're hooking everything up at once. If things go easy for you, this is the worst you'll have it in this room."

He slid another band over Robert's head; it held two straws that he placed in his nostrils. "Breathe through those the whole time." They smelled like the inside of a box of latex gloves.

"This next part is the most invasive, but it's no worse than a little acupuncture."

"No problem," Robert bluffed.

Marcus shaved a few spots on Robert's arms and chest and then slid tiny wires into the muscles. After the initial poke, it looked weirder than it felt.

"Ok, now I'm gonna put these headphones on you and you won't be able to hear me anymore. A bunch of pictures are going to display on that monitor right there, and all you have to do is stay as calm as you can, breathe through the tubes, and don't close your eyes or look away or we'll have to start over. Got it?" Robert was pretty sure he was already making all the monitors he was attached to spike or bounce or whatever it was he wasn't supposed to be making them do. He nodded.

Marcus started the test. At first Robert heard gentle music and the screen showed pictures of forest paths and beaches and cute domestic animals. Each image stayed up for about ten seconds. Robert braced himself. He knew some disturbing shit was coming. That was the point, to provoke a stress reaction, and it started after maybe a minute or two: a giant spider, an open wound, thrown in among the waterfalls and baby goats.

The music picked up, growing less melodic and more chaotic. The pictures became more skewed toward the disturbing: a face that was half tumor, the aftermath of a dog fight, a pile of dead and rotting pigs swarming with insects, naked napalm victims. Ten long seconds of every image. Robert tried to dissociate from his vision, to see the screen but focus on breathing and relaxing the tension that gripped his muscles.

What came through the headphones wasn't even music anymore, just clanging and scratching and howling. There were more images of violence, of bruised and battered faces, of a bull dragging his intestines behind him in the dirt, of a man being sodomized with a baseball bat. Dozens of traumatic, gory images. He forgot all about breathing and relaxing. He just kept counting to ten, hoping the next picture would be less disturbing. And every once in a while, among the starving children, the fresh landmine victims, the mass graves, there would be a respite: a flower, a rainbow, a school of fish. Finally the ratio returned in the favor of beauty, softness. The music regained its order.

Marcus stepped forward from where Robert had forgotten he'd been standing. "It's over," he said as he removed the headphones.

"Damn," was all Robert could manage.

"Yeah, but by the time you're finished in this room, you won't react to any of that. You'll be on an even keel no matter what's put in front of you."

Robert put it together that this was why everyone had been so easygoing at lunch. If they'd been trained not to react to piles of dead bodies, one moron stumbling through the line without any tact certainly wasn't going to upset them.

"Most people usually want to lie down for a while after their sessions. We can get your neurophage baseline tomorrow."

"Yeah, that sounds like a good idea," Robert said in a daze. He shuffled back to his room and eased himself into the chair. He must have stared at the wall for almost an hour, because next thing he knew it was time to meet Johnnie. Busy day.

17
HAND JIVE

"**H**EY ROBBIE, first biofeedback is intense huh?" Johnnie said as Robert staggered into the courtyard.

"Yeah. Intense."

"Still want to hear about the trepanation procedure?"

"Yes. I do."

"Ok," he said. "But there really isn't much to it. You just go in, get numbed up, and they punch your hole."

"It doesn't hurt?"

"You hardly feel anything. Nothing at all compared to some of the shit I've been through." Johnnie picked up his mangled right hand and fluttered his fingers at Robert, who was too tired to hide his fascination. "Wanna hear about that? It's a much better story."

"Sure," Robert said.

"All right, cool. This is a good one." And Johnnie was off.

"So I was 19 and a total fucking hooligan, a real shit. One of those kids with all the questions. Why are we here? Why is everyone so lame? How can I not be like them? I tried real hard to be *punk fucking rock*—vandalizing, shoplifting, getting fucked up, going to shows. That's what I thought it meant to go against the norm and, you know, push boundaries and shit.

"It wasn't though, you know. I wasn't going against the norm. Not really. Not yet.

"Ok so, this happened when I was going to drop off a few kilos of weed on the other side of the city with my friend Jesus. We were in his old white van. And I mean *old*, old. Damn, did he love that van. Kept it spotless. Had a chamois in the back and would buff its chrome bumpers and headlights and old metal side mirrors whenever he got the chance.

"Right, so the tape deck was playing The Cramps, 'Mama mama oo pow pow,' and I had my arm resting on the door, you know, tapping out the rhythm in the open space where the window was rolled-down. Now Jesus was just about the slowest motherfucker on the face of the earth. Not like stupid slow, but like turtle slow. So, Jesus takes a left turn with the green light, a leading left arrow, right? Now, he's moving practically in slow motion because, I mean first off, he just lives that way, but also, two, because the van is fucking old, and three, the back is full of pot and he's hella paranoid. So, we're hardly moving at all and the light must have changed because here comes this fucking burgundy K-car heading right for us.

"This guy in the Chrysler, this meth head, he just saw green means go you know. Didn't expect a solid metal brick in his path. He *slammed* into the van's shiny right front bumper. I was thrown forward and jerked back. I totally remember it in slow motion, maybe because I was pretty high at the time. With the forward momentum, right, the chromed-out side mirror support slices right between these two fingers here, my middle finger and my ring finger. Then all the sudden I'm yanked back, minus the strip of flesh that was left hanging from the metal brace. All the major tendons and ligaments and shit that held my hand together were ripped in half, right down to the bones at the base of my hand, almost to the wrist.

"The van was still running, so we didn't wait around for the cops. I wrapped my hand in my shirt and we dropped off the load. Then I went to the ER, but I didn't have insurance, so no way could I afford the reconstructive surgery they wanted to do to put my hand back together. Instead they just sewed it up along the gouged-out edges." Johnnie held his hand up and gave a grossly exaggerated Vulcan salute.

"Ironic I guess you could say," Johnnie went on. "I've always been into sideshows and freaks. Not interested so much in the 'deformities,'" he made air quotes, "as much as people being able to make a living off of simply existing. I mean, some girl goes into premature menopause, gains a shit load of weight and grows a beard, and now all she has to do is sit around and not shave? What is that life like? To have your identity sealed like that—Bearded Lady, Conjoined Twin, Wolf Boy, Four-Legged Girl.

"Now I was, in a way, like them. My identity problem was solved. There was no fucking way I was gonna be mistaken for normal anymore. Shaking hands, getting change, making out. We do a lot of interacting with our hands.

"I've had decades of experience now watching how people change when they see a disfigurement. It's amazing how many people's humanity really is that superficial. It was only after the accident that I really started to push the boundaries, know what I mean?"

Still shell shocked from the biofeedback, Robert looked at Johnnie's hand, at his tattoos and scars and implants and at the hole in the middle of his third-eye tattoo. And he said, "If you were going to kill yourself, how would you do it?"

Without missing a beat, and with a big grin on his illustrated face, Johnnie Curseword said, "I'd pitch myself off a skyscraper into a parade."

18
JUST A HAIR OVER AVERAGE

THE NEXT DAY, Marcus took Robert to a room in the white wing that was dominated by a giant imaging machine. This was the test his state insurance didn't cover. Robert laid on the padded table and was slid into a tube.

"Just be really still. Breathe normal," Marcus said, then he went into the adjoining room, tucking himself away behind a wall of glass, safe from the barrage of radiation.

In an unbidden image, Robert pictured the screens Marcus was watching growing crowded with bugs made of green light, signifying his multiplicity of brain mites, the overpopulated colony in his head. The longer he lay there the more he could feel them, see them, feeding, growing bigger, getting bloated. What if they ate too much? Would they split open? Explode?

"Calm your breathing," Marcus said through a speaker. "We're almost done." Robert focused on slowing down his breath until it was over. As Marcus pressed the button to make the bed slide out, he said, "Your count is just a hair over average."

Days passed and Robert still hadn't heard from Bet. He'd seen her car in the parking lot, so he knew she was there somewhere. The only parts of the building he hadn't been yet were the operating room and the South Wing, so he assumed she was in the latter.

Wherever she was, not seeing her gave his brain more time to play ping pong with his decision to come to Forato House. If his bug count was just above average, and not astronomical like he'd thought, then his obsession with brain mites was entirely self-created. And if this was the case, would trepanation really solve his obsession? The idea of drilling a hole in his head to let the bugs out was looking pretty insane. Then again, if getting rid of them meant getting rid of his depression, it would still be worth it. But his rampant insecurity told him this wasn't the place for him. This was a place for risk takers, like Johnnie Curseword, and for people seeking higher states of consciousness, whatever that meant. Then again, whenever he thought about leaving, he remembered Bet. If he left, he'd be letting her down. He'd be a disappointment to her, and to himself, again. She'd leave. She'd probably take the cat. He'd be alone again. Wallowing in his depressive self-pity again. Suicidal again. So he stayed. If things didn't work out here, he could always kill himself later. Maybe he was just on a different path to the same end, but at least this way there was a small chance it was a path to a different end.

He went through the days: breakfast, biofeedback, lunch, afternoons spent reading or talking with Johnnie, dinner, reading, lucid dreaming exercises, sleep, begin again.

19
DREAMING OF KATHERINE

ROBERT THREW BACK the sheets and sat up. He pressed the heels of his hands into his eyes.

He had failed at lucid dreaming, again. Now it was important, he'd been told, to remember the dream before it faded.

He'd been standing outside his apartment door, and it occurred to him that Bet was inside. The thought made him smile. He reached for the doorknob, focusing in on his hand. It was a lucid dreaming device, a trick, to use seeing your hands as a reminder to tell yourself, "I'm dreaming. This is *my* dream. I'm in charge and can do whatever I want."

Robert was pleased he'd remembered to look at his hand. Things were going well.

He opened the door. Something was wrong. The small apartment was stacked high with glossy magazines. He knew without looking that there would be *Cosmo* and *Vogue* and *Elle*, *Surface* and *Aesthetica*. They were Katherine's favorites. But why would Katherine's things be here? He was confused.

Then he saw her. She was on the bed, lying on her stomach with her elbows propping her up. She flipped the pages of a magazine, her Mary Janes in the air and pleated plaid skirt barely reaching her thighs.

"Where have you been?" Katherine asked without looking up.

"Um. I've been at Forato House?"

"What a waste," she said. "They can't fix you. You're so broken, no one can fix you."

Katherine sat cross-legged now. She wasn't wearing anything under her short skirt.

"You're a waste of space, Robert. Shouldn't you be taking control? Shouldn't you be morphing me into that carnie chick you're crushing on? You can't do it, can you? You know why? Because you're weak. You've got no guts, Robert. If you did, you wouldn't be such a drag to be around."

Robert didn't argue, didn't ask her to leave, didn't do anything but stand there and take the abuse. It was all true. He was a waste of space. He wasn't even strong enough to take control of his own dream.

"I don't know what I ever saw in you," Katherine went on. "I've never seen anyone do less in a day. You have no ambition, no talent. It must have been pity. But a girl can only take so much moping and self-loathing. I'm glad I got out of here when I did."

She stood up from the bed and something grayish-white fell from between her legs. It was an inch long and looked like a beetle larva. And then another and another fell out. As she walked toward where Robert was standing, still in front of the door, the flow gained momentum, until beetle larvae gushed out from under her skirt, until the two of them were ankle deep in fat, slimy, wriggling sacs.

Robert looked closer and saw that they were not beetle larvae at all; they were tardigrades, giant water bear-brain mites, squirming and climbing over each other to get to him.

Done squirting his worst fear from her vagina, Katherine took Robert by the shoulders and slid him aside so she could get to the door.

Robert felt water bears squish under his feet as he moved. He felt them cling to his legs and start climbing. He felt the cold sweat and pounding pulse that signaled the onset of a panic attack.

"I'm coming with you," he said.

Katherine looked at him the way the mean girl looks at the final girl at the beginning of the slasher flick—you don't get it and I don't care.

"You can't leave your own brain, dumbass," she said.

Katherine slammed the door behind her, leaving Robert alone in a six-inch-deep writhing mass of brain mites. He tried to take a step toward the door but couldn't. Hundreds of bugs were clinging to his feet and ankles, and others crawled over those and attached themselves higher up, and others still crawled over *those*—they built layer on top of layer, flaring out from his knees, creating cones that attached him to the floor. On and on they climbed and crawled and covered him. Robert watched horrified as his legs disappeared under the repulsive hoard.

That is when the panic woke him up.

She was right. Everything Katherine said in the dream, all that vile, acrimonious poison, it was all true. He was no one to anyone. He was a shell and a sham of a person, going through the motions of life because he was afraid to do anything else.

Maybe today he'd steal a knife from the cafeteria. Or he could use his sheets to make a noose and hang himself from the giant mesquite tree in the center of the courtyard. There were plenty of ways to kill yourself, even in a place like this.

20
NIGHT VISIT

IT WAS LATE in the evening. Bet stood outside the door to her dad's room, glancing furtively up and down the hallway. She knocked. No answer. She used her key card and opened the door, closing it quickly behind her. He wasn't there. Shit. She couldn't chance going into the common areas. If anybody saw her, she'd be fired for sure.

Tap, tap. There was just the faintest knock on Robert's door. He heard a card swipe unlock it. The door opened and closed quickly, and where there was nothing just a moment before, now there was Bet.

He jumped out of bed, moving toward her. He wanted to touch her. To tell her he'd missed her. Instead, he stopped in the middle of the room. "Bet."

"Hi Rob." She smiled.

"What are you doing here? Is everything ok? Have you talked to your dad yet? Does he know you're here?" It all came out in a rush.

"I'm fine. Everything is fine. Calm down. This is just the first time I could get away."

She moved toward him, past him, and sat on the bed. He sat on the chair and scooched it closer to her. He should have moved it first. He was sure he looked ridiculous holding on to the arms and thrusting, scraping the chair over the thin carpet, until their knees almost touched.

"I just wanted to see you," she said. "I shouldn't be here. I could lose my job. Then it would be up to you to get my dad out of here. I just went by his room but he wasn't there. You've talked to him? How is he? Have you told him I'm here?"

"I haven't. I was waiting to hear from you. He's really into all of this. I think it's like an amusement park for him—no worries, free trips. It won't be easy to get him to leave."

"I figured as much. I'm so glad you're here, and not just to convince him. It's nice to know I'm not alone." Bet smiled again, this time, for the first time, a little shy. She reached out and took Robert's hand. She looked right into his eyes and asked, "I can count on you, right?"

His heart fell into his stomach. He still didn't know why he was here—for love or for bugs.

"Of course. Anything. I would do anything for you."

And then there was one of those moments, one of those we're-going-to-kiss-now-right? kind of moments. Robert leaned forward, but Bet pulled back. Maybe he'd read the situation wrong. Wouldn't be the first time. The way she was looking at him, he'd seen it before. She was looking at him like he was crazy. He'd seen it every time he'd told anyone he'd been seeing a psychiatrist off and on since the third grade. Her eyes were full of questions and fear but also curiosity. Then her look changed from questioning to consequences-be-damned, and she kissed him. A lot.

She slid onto his lap. After a minute or two or who knows how long, Robert certainly couldn't tell, he asked, "Are we going to . . . Do you want to . . . ?"

"Yes," she said.

21
THE GIRL WITH THE HOLE IN HER HEAD

"**D**ID I EVER tell you about how I discovered trepanation?" Johnnie asked.

It was the next afternoon and Robert and Johnnie were sitting outside, in the shade of the mesquite trees. Johnnie had to speak up so Robert could hear him over the electric buzz of the cicada.

"It was through a girl. Not a girl, a woman, named Charlie. The beautiful, amazing, Charlotte Dunn—the girl with the hole in her head. Charlie's asshole ex-girlfriend hit her in the head with a hammer. She told me she woke up on the kitchen floor, blood everywhere, so she called 911. At the hospital they took out the shattered chunks of bone and sewed up her scalp. She said she noticed a difference as soon as the shock wore off.

"And the difference she described sounded like magic to me. She said all of her senses were sharper, totally fucking in focus. She said not only was she aware of every leaf on every tree, but she could feel the trees pulsing with life. She said when she washed her hands she could feel the history of the water. When people spoke—to her, to other people, on the radio—she knew what they really meant, not just what they were saying.

"She said her life started with that hole in her head.

"Charlie was the most down-to-earth, awake person I ever met. Not afraid, not jaded, just totally fascinated by whatever came her way. She was alive. It didn't hurt that she was fucking gorgeous, or that she kept the left half of her head buzzed to show off her indentation. So hot. Damn man, imagine sex with someone that aware? Holy shit.

"I wanted to be like Charlie. So I started looking for someone to put a hole in my skull. No one in the body-modification scene would touch it. I had a guy with dyed black eyes—whites, irises, everything black—tell me I was crazy to even be thinking about it.

"So I thought fuck it then, I'll just do it myself. I trained with a piercer. I even bought a drill. A regular drill, not like the expensive drill they have here. But when it came down to it, I couldn't do it. I'd been right-handed before the accident and I wasn't sure I could stop with my left hand before drilling into my brain. So I kept looking for someone who would trepan me. I found Halvorson's medical tourism offer, but I couldn't get a passport because of the time I was busted with a shitload of MDMA. And then Charlie herself told me about Forato House and the brain mite experiment. About how they would make the hole if you agreed to participate in their study with hallucinogens. She followed this up with, 'You know, a lot of what happened to me, my changes, could have been from escaping that abusive relationship and surviving a near-death experience. It might not have been the hole at all.'

"But as soon as she mentioned Project Skylight, I was already signed up. This was the answer. The whole hallucinogens-shot-directly-into-your-brain thing is just a bonus. I don't give a shit about brain mites. I figure they're just like all the billions of other little bugs living all over us. All I cared about was getting trepanned.

"But I was going to need some money. So I told my daughter I needed help paying for rehab." Robert raised an eyebrow. "Ah man, don't judge. Yes, I lied to her, but only because I was dead certain that if I did this, I'd never have to ask her for anything ever again. A hole in the head and all would be well."

"Johnnie," Robert said, "There's something I should have told you when we first met, about your daughter." And he vomited it all out, about Bet being there and wanting to get Johnnie to leave, about being in love with her, about her thinking he was there to help her, and about him really wanting to do the experiment but not telling her that because he didn't want to let her down.

When he finally stopped talking, Johnnie said, "Huh. Cool."

22
THE SOUTH WING

THE DAYS KEPT passing, bringing Robert closer to getting a hole drilled in his forehead. Each day was a lot like the one before, until one of those days was different.

Robert had spent the morning in biofeedback training playing a video game that taught him to stabilize his high beta brain waves. And he spent the afternoon listening to Johnnie rue the passing of freak shows.

"Why not? Why not let these folks get together, travel around, and have people pay to gawk at them? But no. Instead they have to work at K-Mart and get paid minimum wage for the same thing. Only it's worse without their freak-show brethren, without the banners and talkers telling the world that they're spectacular, mind-blowing, one-of-a-kind."

Johnnie would have joined a freak show in a second. "I was totally down to be the next Lobster Boy. Hang out with other outcasts, travel around fleecing people. Dude, dream job." But there were no traveling freak shows. "It's all about anti-discrimination and integration and shit. Where's the fun in that?"

Later, in the early evening, Robert heard a tentative knock at his door. Bet let herself in. It had been a few days since he'd seen her, since they'd been together. In the interim, given any downtime at all his mind would replay the details. It was a welcome, if occasionally embarrassing, reprieve from obsessing about brain bugs.

"Come with me," she said. "There's something I want you to see."

Not a repeat of last time then. His half-mast lowered.

"What's going on?" he asked.

"There's something I need to show you. I probably should have last time, but, honestly, I needed to know you were with me, all the way. I've been using your laptop and I accidentally saw your browser history. I promise I wasn't snooping. But I did start to think maybe you weren't here just to help me with my dad."

"Bet—," he started to say.

"It's ok. Come on. We don't have much time."

She led him down the East Hall and through the white door into the world of white tile. They went further than he'd gone before, eventually turning right again into the South Wing. They came up against another door blocking the hall. This one said "AUTHORIZED PERSONNEL ONLY."

Bet swiped her card and pushed open the door. Robert recognized it immediately. It was a psych ward. The one place in the world he swore he would never go back to. He would kill himself before going back. He'd spent hours thinking of how. He could have choked himself on drain cleaner, jumped off a cliff, set himself on fire, sliced through his jugular vein, taken a bath with a toaster, run out in front of a semi on the highway. He could be dead in a dozen different ways, but here he was. With Bet.

"This is where I work," she said.

It wasn't exactly like the ward he'd been in. It was a compressed version of it, all in one room—hospital beds with privacy dividers, an empty nurse's station, and, at the far end, a miniature day room complete with vinyl couches and plastic chairs.

Everything inside him was screaming, *run*! But he stumbled after Bet, tripping over his own feet.

"This is Joaquin," Bet said, nodding toward a young man sitting on the end of the bed closest to them. Joaquin had an enormous smile and a hole in his forehead.

He spoke quickly. "Hello. Hi. What's happening? How do you know Bet? Thank you for coming to visit. We don't get visitors here. We aren't supposed to. We're a secret. You shouldn't be here. But we promised Bet we wouldn't squeal. She's great, isn't she? Charles said not to worry about it."

"Hello Joaquin. Good to meet you," Robert said.

Bet wrapped her arm in Robert's and he calmed down. It was an easy gesture on her part, showing they were together, he was under her protection.

She led him to the next bed, saying, "And this is Francis. He doesn't talk much."

Francis was hard to look at. His whole body was slack, propped up in the bed. His eyes were vacant, his head hung awkwardly on his shoulder, and his mouth gaped open. Bet left Robert's side to dab away a string of drool that dribbled onto the catatonic man's chest. Robert glanced around the room, needing to look anywhere but at Francis. There were maybe eight people in there, mostly men but also a couple of women, and almost all of them had a hole, but one or two did not.

"What is this place?" he asked Bet.

"Hold on. Here's Charles. Charles can tell you better than I can." She led him by the hand into the day room. The couches and chairs faced the wall, on the other side of which must have been the reception room. This was the end of the square that made up Forato House. The TV was off, so the object of focus was a nature mural, made to look like the view out of a window.

"Charles, this is my friend Robert."

Charles was a stocky old man with dark skin and a knit cap. He looked right at Robert. "The sex was that good, huh?"

Robert coughed and swallowed hard. He looked at Bet.

"Charles is very intuitive," she said. "It's ok. You can ask him your questions. But make it quick, the nurse will be back soon."

"Ok," he tried to brush off Charles's very intuitive comment, "What is this place? Why are you all here?"

"We are here, most of us, because the experiment worked. See Joaquin down there? Not a brain mite in there. He so fucking happy, there's no way he could live out in the world. No fear. All trust. And Daniel over here? He's perfectly content ninety-nine percent of the time. But because he came to us with PTSD, and we didn't know any better, sometimes he gets trapped in hallucinations. Then he'll rampage, thinking he's still fighting the bugs." All three of them looked over at Daniel, who gave them a half smile and went back to his book. "Looks fine now, but when the flashbacks happen, he has to be completely restrained. Broke Big Angus's leg here just a week ago." He indicated a large man with a bright blue cast.

Robert felt an urgent need to get as much information, as many pieces of the puzzle, as he could before he had to leave. If the experiment was as safe as Arianne made it out to be, why did this room even exist? If they were all here because the experiment worked, why were they all acting so differently from one another? Francis was basically comatose and Charles appeared to be completely normal, if creepily perceptive.

"What about Francis?" he asked. "Or you?"

"Well, Francis has obviously reached the highest state, nirvana, the pinnacle of peace on earth."

Bet tugged on his arm. "We need to go."

"What about you?" he asked Charles.

"Me? I'm here by choice."

Bet tugged again, and this time he followed her. As they left the room, Joaquin waved good-bye with both hands and Charles said, from the far side of the room, "See you again, real soon."

✳✳✳

When they got back to his room, Bet came in and closed the door behind her.

"What the fuck?" was all he could say.

"I know. I know. We have to get my dad out of this place."

"Have you seen him yet?"

"No, I haven't seen him. I'm stuck in that ward all day."

"I told him everything—that you're here, that we're together, that you want him to leave. He didn't jump at it. He didn't have much to say at all. He's so far into the process, he's been on four or five trips already, everything in his world is peaches. But that fucking psych ward you just showed me changes everything. What did Charles mean, they're there because the experiment worked? I need to get back in there, soon. Can you take me back tonight?"

"No way. Maybe tomorrow. If I can."

"How's Theo?" Robert remembered to ask. The question had a grounding effect on the conversation.

"He's great. It's nice to have the company."

Robert wanted to tell her he wished he could be there, too, but he wasn't ready to give up on the experiment, even after what he just saw. Instead, he wished he could split himself in two and live one

68

life where he went home with her and one where he went through with it. But he didn't have two lives, and if he didn't get rid of the brain mites, he might not have any life at all. That thing happened where their eyes connected, and what he saw in hers made him feel embarrassed and guilty. He broke contact.

She took both of his hands, stood on her tiptoes, and kissed him.

23
THE DANIEL INCIDENT

ARIANNE STOOD IN the first rays of dawn. She hadn't seen this coming. This could seriously derail her plans.

The police cars still had their lights on. An EMT closed the back doors of an ambulance and ran to hop into the passenger seat. It took off down the dirt road, a dust cloud disappearing into the distance. Another gurney rolled past them, its passenger completely covered with a sheet. This crew moved less urgently, making their way to a second ambulance.

"It appears he took the key card from the nurse's station," the detective said, flipping through her small notepad.

The night nurse, Hector, had always been reliable. But there were any number of reasons he might have fallen asleep at the tail end of his shift.

"He used the card to get into the operating room, where he found a scalpel and stabbed the chair in there—" she flipped to the second page and back to the first, "apparently over a hundred times." The detective paused for Arianne to make a comment. She didn't.

"After that he made his way to the kitchen. He found one staff member, Gabriel Hernandez, alone. Slit his throat, looks like from behind since there was no struggle. He found the two women together. Stabbed one, Andrea Wells, while he grabbed the other, Maria Vargas, around the neck. He continued to stab Ms. Wells several times. Ms. Vargas managed to bite his arm and get away. She's the one who called us."

Yes she did, Arianne thought. She must remember to talk to that one later. Procedure is to call for in-house security first, avoid all this attention. Now there would be a fuss. At the least there would be an official record of the event with the police and probably in the local paper. At the worst it would be picked up by regional or even national news, the spectacle *du jour* on the internet. This was not the national debut she wanted.

"And what will happen to Daniel now?" Arianne asked, the picture of composure. "Will we still have access to him?"

The detective pulled a face, a that's-really-not-the-right-response-to-this-situation kind of face. "Once he's sentenced, he'll be allowed visitors."

"Sentenced? Won't there be a trial?"

"He confessed."

"I see." Arianne refrained from asking if they could argue temporary insanity. If it worked, the blame would shift off of him and onto them, onto her, for negligence, for allowing him access to the key card and the scalpel. For tinkering with his brain. No, Daniel would have to be an unknown martyr to the cause.

"In the meantime," the detective went on, "we're going to have to ask you to shut down. This whole place is a crime scene."

"I'm afraid that's impossible. We're in the middle of an experiment. I have an ethical responsibility to see that these people continue to receive treatment. Releasing them now would be negligent."

"The same experiment Daniel was a part of?'

"No, Daniel was a permanent guest. A patient, not a subject."

"All right. I'll talk to the chief and see if we can work something out. But no one goes into the taped-off areas."

24
SUICIDE BRINGS PEOPLE TOGETHER

ARIANNE CLOSED HER office door. "Please, take a seat. Would you like some tea?"

"No, thank you," Robert answered.

"I used to be just like you, Robert" she said as she went about fixing herself a cup from the electric kettle. She set her mug on the desk but didn't move behind it. This was a time to project reassurance not through power but through similarity. She needed to sew the seams of her plan together as tightly as she could now. She needed to know that Robert was with her.

Standing in front of him, she pulled back the loose sleeve of her kaftan, showing Robert the long shiny scars that ran up the inside of her forearm. She could tell by his wide eyes that this wasn't what he'd been expecting. "And after that, I rested my head in a gas oven. And after that I took sleeping pills and tied a plastic bag over my head."

She angled the second guest chair to face him and sat down. "And each time, Charles found me."

At the mention of Charles, Robert tensed. "Yes, I know," Arianne said, trying to put him at ease. "And I know about you and the housekeeper who took you to see him, too. Charles and I have been together since, well, for a long, long time."

Robert stammered like a student in the principal's office, "Look, I'm really sorry. I know I wasn't supposed to go back there. I haven't told anybody."

"Don't worry, Robert. You're not in trouble. Just the opposite, actually." Arianne took a sip of her tea. "You're more important than you know."

"What do you mean, important?"

"Let me start at the beginning. Like I said, I was a lot like you. Every time Charles saved my life, I started scheming new ways to get rid of it. But Charles wasn't giving up on me. He made sure I went to therapy, took my Prozac, made all the right 'lifestyle choices.'" She made air quotes around the phrase. "But it wasn't enough. So we started experimenting—What about speed? A little cocaine? Microdosing LSD?

"Some of it helped and some only made it worse. He kept careful records of everything. And well, you know how it goes, we were headed down the rabbit hole, and you meet some mighty strange people down there. One of them told us about trepanation.

"At first we were skeptical, to say the least. But then I had a bad relapse. I stayed in bed for days. When I was awake, I could only weep. I didn't speak. I didn't eat. I wouldn't even drink water. I was done. Done trying, done experimenting, done constantly fighting for my life. I was going to let myself waste away. And then Charles brought the drill into the bedroom. Of course I thought he was mad! Stark, raving insane. Would this man really go to any lengths to keep me from killing myself? It's my life. Let me end it if I want to! I remember telling him 'No,' through my dry mouth, my cracked lips, and raising my hand to cover my forehead. 'It's not for you,' he told me. 'At least, not yet.' And he set up shop and trepanned himself right there in front of me."

Arianne paused, stirring her tea.

"God, was that a gory sight," she said, her eyes for the first time not watching Robert for his reaction. "Anyway," she shook the bloody memory away, "The difference it made in him was profound. He'd always been thoughtful and kind, but now his level of awareness was nearly superhuman. It was as if all of his senses had expanded. After a few days, when he asked if I was ready, I said yes."

"Wow," Robert said. "You know, I'm ready too. I'm getting better at all the biofeedback stuff. And I've had a couple of good moments with lucid dreaming, too. I mean, I haven't mastered any of it, but I'm really ready."

"I know," she said. "I think you're ready too. But that's not where the story ends. Let me tell you the rest.

"Before anybody even knew about brain mites, Charles and I were experimenting. We bought this place and started doing public studies on biofeedback and using LSD to treat alcoholism and things like that. But when we had free time, we experimented on ourselves, shooting different drugs directly into our brains. We were careful. As careful as we could be. We introduced a paralytic, so we couldn't hurt ourselves or anyone else. We used small doses, and only one of us would be under at a time. It was fun. It was intense. We tried all kinds of combinations. At first the trips were full of bugs and bogeymen. But with the right drugs and the right frame of mind, they were easily defeated.

"When the bugs were gone, not only did we find our psyches well balanced, our moods lifted, our sex amazing," she smiled just a little, "but with the right combination of hallucinogens, something brand new happened. We met our gods."

Arianne grew more animated now. "I met Shiva. Charles met Jah. The gods that we had pictured. At first I figured they were just our inner representations, our superegos anthropomorphized or something like that. But eventually we started to see things, to know things. You met Charles, so you have some idea what I'm talking about. He's become deeply intuitive—not quite telepathic, but damn near it. And, you probably won't believe this, but I can see the future. Well, I can see potential futures."

She paused. Robert was looking at the wall, the floor, anywhere but at her.

"I know," she said. "I know it sounds crazy. Charles is much better proof than me. But think about it, Robert. Think about what this means. It's a whole new level of human evolution. We've found a way to unlock each individual's greatest potential. And you're the key, Robert. I've seen it. You're going to be the one to take this to the public, to sell it to the world!"

Robert's eyes were wide, and when he opened his mouth no sound came out.

"Too soon. I know. I didn't want to drop it all on you like this. But, well, you heard about what happened with Daniel?"

"I did."

"Please understand that when Daniel went through Project Skylight, we didn't know what we know now. He didn't have the training that you do. He wasn't ready for what he saw in there. It's only with the sacrifice of people like Daniel and the others you met in the South Wing that we've been able to perfect the experiment. I wish it could have been otherwise."

Arianne paused here and looked into her tea. She hoped she appeared contrite.

"Anyway," she went on, "I feel like we really need to move things along now. We could be getting some unwanted attention soon. So, how would you like to get your trepanation today?"

25
MOM

ROBERT'S MOTHER HUGGED him twice a day. The first hug was when he got home from school. He'd walk in the front door of their little condo and head straight for the couch where she made her nest. She'd scooch to the edge of the light blue cushion and hold out her arms. He would walk into them and she would hold him. She smelled like shampoo and beer and cigarettes. Sometimes she would cry. She never asked how his day went. She never told him to stay with her or to go play. She just held him and then went back to watching TV.

The second hug was at night, before bed. She smelled less like shampoo then, and more like vodka or rum. The cigarette smell was the same. The goodnight hug was shorter. Dad was there. Dad, who always walked hunched in on himself, who always looked like he needed sleep. Robert never saw her hug Dad the way she hugged him.

He remembered thinking as a kid that the afterschool hug was longer because to her, she'd made it through one more day. "You're my reason for living," she'd told him one time. "It's harder for me when you aren't around." That hug embodied all of her relief. Her reason for living was home again.

Mom had everything she needed in her nest on the couch. She was surrounded by blankets and pillows; cigarettes, lighter, and ashtray; boxes of tissues; her little amber pill bottles; the TV remote; and stacks of magazines Dad bought her from the grocery store. The magazines were all about celebrities and TV, *Us* and *People* and *TV Guide*. She watched TV all day, so he was trying to give her something she'd be interested in. But inside the covers, Mom drew horns and goatees on the men, fangs and bat wings on the women. Some people, some whole pages, she inked in, turning them completely black. She wrote words Robert wasn't supposed to say and some he didn't recognize over people's faces: *bitch, cunt, fuckhead*. She never stopped him from looking at them.

It wasn't that she didn't care what he did. "As long as you're happy, I could give a shit about anything else," she told him.

And then one day he got off the bus at the same time Grandma was pulling into the driveway. Grandma never came over during the week. He ran to catch up with her and walked into the house right behind her. Mom's nest was empty, and so were the plastic pill and glass liquor bottles all around the couch.

Grandma said, "I'm sorry I didn't get here sooner to get these things cleared up." And she hugged him, but it wasn't the right kind of hug.

Robert and Dad moved in with Grandma soon after Mom's funeral. Within days Dad started to change. He smiled. He told jokes. He was relieved, Robert could tell. Relieved that he didn't have Mom dragging him down anymore. Relieved that he didn't have to worry about her or take care of her all the time. Mom had been broken beyond fixing, and people like that make life hard for everyone around them. Robert didn't accuse Dad of not loving Mom, of not grieving enough. He just decided to grieve enough for everyone.

He built his own nest on the couch. Blankets and pillows; chips and sodas; the TV remote. He spent every minute he could in his nest, mourning his mom. Eventually they made him see a counselor who said he needed sunshine and fruit instead of TV and junk food. He did what they told him to, and he always heard the silent *you don't want to end up like your mother, do you?* after their instructions. "Go play outside, *you don't want to end up like your mother, do you?*" "Here, have an apple. *You don't want to end up like your mother, do you?*" And they were right. He didn't want to. Because if he was like her, he'd be a burden, a disappointment, and they'd be happy when he died.

So Robert tried. He rode his bike aimlessly just so he wouldn't be at home. He ate what they put in front of him. He read instead of watching TV. And it worked. The counselor said he had recovered from his grief. Now he was just a normal, if introverted, kid. Dad and Grandma were relieved, and Robert kept faking it. He didn't want to disappoint them. He faked his way through middle school. He faked his way through the first two years of high school. Then Grandma passed away. She went quietly, in her sleep. And that is when Dad grieved, when something broke inside of him that was never put right again. It made him hollow, and then Dad found out what it meant to live life just going through the motions.

Broken people aren't grieved and real grieving breaks people. There's no way to win. Death is inevitable. Better to do it when you're alone in the world, when there's no one to disappoint and no one to break.

❈❈❈

Robert was tired of being down, of being so down that all he could think about was how down he was. He was tired of feeling as if the longer he lived, the more of a disappointment he was going to be to himself and everyone around him. He was tired of all of it. He'd been there for too many years. He'd spent his whole life in this flat, dull world.

And then there was Bet. Bet lifted the fog. With her, he'd had a glimpse of a life worth living.

But he wasn't stupid. He knew better than to pin his hopes on somebody, anybody, else. No, that was beyond wishful thinking, that was unfair. He couldn't put someone else under that kind of pressure, being responsible for his happiness.

To have any chance at a life worth living, any chance of being with her, he had to fix himself. And from what he'd seen, between Johnnie and the other Project Skylight participants, it worked. At least, it made them happy. What happened to the people in the South Wing, what happened with Daniel, that was all tragic. But he believed Arianne. He believed Project Skylight would save him.

26
ROBERT'S TREPANATION

THE CHAIR **ROBERT** was strapped into had dozens of knife holes in it. It was covered in plastic, like everything else in the operating room.

Arianne reclined the chair with a foot pedal. "This'll be just a pinch here," she said as she injected the anesthetic into his forehead. "Oh, and here's Doctor David now." They heard the door open and a tall man entered Robert's field of vision. All Robert could see of him were watery blue eyes between a face mask and surgeon's cap. "He's been with us a long time. He has a hole of his own," she said.

"Sure do. If I wasn't scrubbed in, I'd show you." He waved his gloved hands at Robert.

"A long time, huh?" Robert said through his teeth. "So, have you met your god? Do you have powers or insight or whatever?"

"I knew you were going to ask that." He winked. "You look ready."

"I am."

"Ok, let's do it."

Doctor David picked up a scalpel. Robert felt the line of the circle the doctor traced in his forehead. He felt him scrape and peel away the skin. Arianne reached in to swab the blood. The doctor extended his arm out of Robert's view to pick up the drill. That's when they heard the door open, again.

"Put it down!" It was Bet's voice.

Arianne and the doctor turned to look at her. Robert tried to look, too, but the straps holding his head were too tight.

79

"Put it down and step back," she said. Dr. David did what she asked.

When Bet was closer, Robert could see she had a chef's knife.

He could feel blood running down from his forehead into his hair, his eyes, his ears.

"Come on Rob. Let's go."

"Bet, it's ok. This is what I want," he said. Blinking away the blood, he followed her with his eyes as she moved in a circle around him, releasing the restraints that held him to the chair. She was holding the knife in front of her and forcing the others to back away from them.

Without taking her attention off of Arianne and the doctor, Bet said, "I can't let you do it. I can't take the chance you'll end up like Daniel, or Francis."

Robert swung his legs off the side of the dentist chair and set his feet on the floor next to the surgical tray. "I'm sorry Bet. I have to do this, as much for you as for me." He picked up the drill and lined up its dime-sized crown-shaped bit with his best guess of where his skin was missing. He closed his eyes and pulled the trigger, pushing the drill into his head and his head into the drill. He felt pressure and then a pop. Inside his skull he felt a release and a short gush. He heard a burbling sound as fluid shifted.

Robert set the drill down and wiped the blood from his eyes. Blood spatter had whirled around the room. Bet had some on her face. She stared at him for few long seconds. Then, as if she had finally processed what happened, she said, "Help him." But Arianne and the doctor were still frozen.

She yelled at them, "Help him!" Blood was pouring down his face now, and a quarter inch of his brain was exposed to the outside world, but Robert felt fine. More than fine, he was relieved, elated, content. It was done.

Arianne and Doctor David laid him back on the chair and started cleaning away the blood, getting ready to install the tunnel. Bet put the knife down on the surgical tray and picked up Robert's hand.

"It's ok," he said. "It really is."

SHIVA'S THIRD EYE 27

THAT NIGHT AS she lay in bed, Arianne was restless. For the first time in a long time, she was uncertain. Daniel's rampage, Bet's interruption of Robert's procedure: why hadn't she seen these things coming? Had she been neglecting her own inner life as Project Skylight got traction? Did she need to take a trip to get her bearings? At the very least it would give her some respite from the Daniel situation—the press, the phone calls, the worried staff. She hadn't had a moment's clear thought since it happened. She decided to go under first thing in the morning.

Arianne approached the mountaintop looking forward to sinking into her seat, losing herself in the flow of all that is, was, or could be. But that was not to be the case today. She knew something was different as soon as she saw Shiva's open eyes.

"Do you know the origin of my third eye?" he asked. His voice was low and its vibrations rumbled through her. She felt something long forgotten, something heavy in her belly. Was this foreboding? Was this fear? She tried to focus on the question. The third eye, where did it come from? Hadn't she heard the story once, a long time ago? From her hippie parents maybe or from their guru?

"I'll remind you," the god said. With every word Arianne felt her insides clench, tightening against the quiet storm of his power.

"Destiny demands certain actions of the gods," he began. "One of these actions was that I take Parvati as my consort. As much as I prefer to stay submerged, to rest below the level of direct involvement with the world and its ongoing tedium, it was my dharma to father children with Parvati.

"She was here with me on this snow-covered peak. We were newly joined. Kartikeya and Ganesha had not yet been born to us, and she was feeling flirtatious. She approached me from behind and covered my eyes." The great god of destruction, whose voice was liquefying Arianne's insides, allowed a brief smile, or maybe a grimace, to cross his face.

"She did not mean any harm by it, just to tease me from my reverie. But the moment her hands covered my eyes, the sun went out. The world was cast into pitch darkness. That is when my third eye emerged. As it opened, it engulfed the world in flames. Within moments, its raw, unrestrained power immolated all of creation.

"Parvati stood shocked at the result of her innocent gesture. When she finally woke, she started to dance. 'Open your eyes,' she said. 'Play your drum for me while I dance.' Smart woman. She knew that the beat of my drum would recreate the heartbeat of creation. The world was made anew."

Shiva let his eyes close. He settled into himself. The silence that followed Shiva's speech was almost as terrible in its emptiness as the sound of his speech had been in its fullness. Arianne had questions but knew she wouldn't get answers from him now. He was submerged again, existing only as a pulse of energy. She took her seat by his side and tried to join him there.

What had he meant? Why tell her that story now? She couldn't let go of the questions. Opening the third eye is enlightenment. Enlightenment brings destruction of false notions. This is what she had been taught, and what she preached to others. But Shiva's third eye burnt down the world. If Shiva couldn't control the power of pure consciousness, how could she? Even more so, how could the children she'd been fostering?

No, she thought, we prepare. We guide. Our intentions are good. But respite from her worries didn't come. Parvati's intentions had been harmless too, and she accidentally destroyed creation.

Arianne's fingers tapped. Her brow creased. These sensations were unfamiliar to her, being unsure, worried, frustrated.

What's done was done. All she could do now was what was best for the future. But try as she might, she could not settle her mind.

She could not slip into that liminal state where all time is now, all space is here, all beings are one.

She waited impatiently for the drugs to wear off.

28
ACCELERATION

SUNSHINE NEVER FELT so good. Robert couldn't stay outside for too long, the sensations were overwhelming. He could feel the individual grains of sand in the concrete bench. The mesquite trees devastated him, so majestic—solid, old, wise. Each fluttering little leaf shimmered its own miraculous presence.

There was life everywhere: ants above and below the ground, cicadas in the trees, Inca doves and Mexican jays squawking and trilling to each other. The blue of the sky was electric. Each cloud a masterpiece, forming, being, dispersing. He had to go inside.

He wandered the halls, the library, touching things as if it were the first time he was seeing this world. He felt the age of the wood in the doors. He mourned the cattle whose skin sheathed the couches. He stood stunned by the mystery of ink on pages translating into human cognition, emotion.

And people! People were amazing. Every genetic accident, every environmental tap on the shoulder, every right and wrong choice that led up to this person, any person, in this moment. The enormity and magic of it! He loved them all.

Johnnie was extra fascinating to watch as they spoke.

"I'm sorry you didn't get to spend time with Bet before she had to leave," Robert told him.

"But I did. She came to talk to me right before she tried to be your hero. Said she wanted me to leave with you and her."

"That must have been hard for you," Robert said, imagining what it would be like for a father to reject his daughter so completely.

"Not really. I told her I'd see her in a couple weeks, when the experiment ends."

There was some food for thought. Was Johnnie not invited to Phase Two? Robert felt a pressing need to talk to Arianne.

"Johnnie," he asked, "how long does the high from the trepanation last?"

"I don't know for sure, just that it lasted the couple of weeks before I started getting the injections. It changes then. It's a hell of a ride though, isn't it?"

Robert had to agree, it was.

✳✳✳

Later that day, Arianne called Robert into her office.

"How are you feeling?" she asked.

"Good, and you know it," he said. "I've got a question for you Arianne. Why is it that Johnnie thinks he's leaving soon? Is he not staying on for Phase Two?" Robert's demeanor was different, more straightforward, almost bold.

"I haven't told him about it yet," she answered. "I haven't told anyone but you. I needed to know that you were on board first. You're the linchpin, Robert. You are the one who holds this all together and propels us into the future—an amazing future. With you at the helm, your story, your believability, and, I know as of yesterday it wouldn't have seemed likely, but your confidence and charisma, we're going to convince an entire generation to join Project Skylight. And when we're done, that generation will raise another generation, an enlightened generation. There will be no more war, no more waste, no more want. I've seen it Robert. It's beautiful. But we need to move quickly. How would you feel about starting the injections early?"

Robert didn't know then that news of Daniel's rampage was all over the internet, or that Forato House was being labeled a drug cult. He didn't know that Bet was sitting in his shitty apartment on his shitty laptop riding that media wave, building a movement against Forato House, against Arianne. Even if he had known, it wouldn't have mattered. He was in love with the world because of Arianne and would say yes to anything she asked for today, no matter how unlikely it was to him that he was about to become the savior of the human race.

29
COLLECTING THE MAIMED

THINGS WERE NOT going Bet's way. Neither of her plans had worked: not the one to get her dad to leave Forato House, nor the one to keep Robert from drilling a hole in his head. She was lucky Arianne hadn't pressed charges. Oddly, she'd done the reverse, oozing generosity, telling Bet there was no need to make a fuss. She was free to go on one condition, she could never come back.

Bet had been fuming mad as she drove back to Robert's apartment. She wasn't used to failure. Stupid men. How could they let someone fuck with their brains? How could they not see the bigger picture? Arianne didn't care about them. She only cared about the experiment. If that woman had an ounce of humanity, there wouldn't be a need for the South Wing. There wouldn't be a need for secrecy. Arianne didn't even care about Daniel or the murders. Two people were dead as a direct result of her meddling with people's minds, and the only thing Arianne did about it was post a guard at the front door. She was more concerned with keeping the press away than with the safety of the people inside. Arianne wasn't being magnanimous when she let Bet go. She did it because calling the cops would have meant more bad press.

By the time Bet was home, she had a new plan. If her dad and Robert couldn't be persuaded to leave on their own, she would just have to bring the whole thing down around them.

She sat down at the desk, pulled Theo onto her lap, and opened Robert's laptop. First, she made a list of all of the people she'd been taking care of and looked up their families and friends. Then she put the word out online that she was looking for anyone who had information about or experiences with Arianne and Forato House. She posted on every site she could find that had anything to do with trepanation, hallucinogens, brain mites, or higher states of consciousness.

Within days Bet was talking with a dozen people—mostly parents and spouses of Arianne's guinea pigs—who each had a story to tell.

"He can't tell the difference between what's real and what isn't anymore."

"She just stares off. When you ask if she's ok, if she's happy, she says yes, and then she goes right back to staring off."

"He'd forget basic hygiene if we didn't remind him. And even then, if anything catches his attention before he makes it to the bathroom, he's likely to shit himself."

The one thing they all had in common was that they were different people when they came out of the experiments than when they went in.

"I wouldn't wish this on my worst enemy. It's like some crucial part of him died in there, the part that made him who he was."

"No, we don't get any kind of support from Forato House. She signed some paperwork saying she wouldn't talk about the experiment, and that she understood the risks and released them from any liability. We've had lawyers look at it. They said it was the real deal, binding or whatever."

Bet had probably signed the same paperwork. She just didn't care. Anyway, there was zero probability that Arianne would bring a case against her and risk exposing what she knew.

The scariest stories came from the few who mentioned more recent changes.

"He's obsessed with car accidents. We were almost hit a few weeks ago and since then he's memorized the statistics of auto accidents in our town, in big cities, in every state, in different countries. He knows the safest cars and where the unsafe ones will buckle and shatter. He knows when and where accidents are most likely to happen. It's all he talks about."

"She's joined the tinfoil hat brigade."

"She had to be committed to keep her from self-harming."

There were some who wrote, who called and said Arianne had saved their lives, that they were miserable until they got the hole, that the experiment gave them the life they always wanted. But there were more who called to find out what they could do, how they could help to put a stop to her.

When Bet told them about the protest, some said they'd do whatever it took to be there. Many, however, demurred. It was too soon, too far, too hard to arrange care and too expensive to travel. She could hear the exhaustion and defeat in their voices. It only fueled her on. She didn't need a lot of people to show up for the next part of her plan to work, even a few would do.

She worked up a press release and sent it to local and national news outfits; newspapers and TV stations; CNN, Buzzfeed, and TMZ. She made a flier and posted it on Facebook and Snapchat and Instagram, asking people to share it. She called Otis at the carnival and enlisted his help in spreading the word.

But what she didn't realize was that for every person who saw her posts online and contacted her with a complaint against Arianne, ten more were looking up the Forato House website and discovering the wonders of trepanation for the first time.

30
MOM, PART TWO

IT WAS RIGHT THERE, sitting across the table from him. A giant tardigrade with an armadillo exoskeleton was sitting on a padded vinyl chair at the faux-wood table where Robert's family used to eat dinner. The bug had to curl in on itself to bring its round mouth full of waving villi down to slurp the spaghetti off its plate, their plates. The ones with the yellow-orange flowers and green vines around the rim.

But it wasn't spaghetti, not really. It was a heaping plate of neurons. Each strand lashing through the air as the giant mite sucked it in. Each elongated cell disappearing into the expressionless creature.

Robert needed to kill it. He looked around for some kind of weapon. He had a fork in his hand. Maybe he could extend it, transform it into something lethal. He focused his attention and watched as the little utensil grew to the size of a pitchfork. The tines were double-edged blades.

Robert turned his attention back to the mite. It had changed. It had eyes now, human eyes. Were they familiar? He stood and took a step toward the hideous thing, holding his giant fork at shoulder height, ready to heave it like a javelin. The bug's mouth was changing, softening. It straightened up and looked at him with those familiar eyes. Robert stopped, waiting to see what it would do.

It didn't approach him. Instead, it left the table and went to the front room, to the couch, changing more with each step, becoming more human. Arms and legs replaced its eight stubby, clawed appendages. It grew hair. By the time it got to the nest on the couch, it was a woman.

It was his mother.

She sat on the couch, curling her legs underneath her and pulling a blanket around her frail body.

"Mom?" he asked.

"Sort of, sweetheart. Come sit with me." He moved slowly, guardedly, setting aside a pile of magazines and sitting down on the light blue cushion. He kept a firm grip on the giant fork.

"What do you mean, 'Sort of?'" he asked.

"I'm what's left of me inside of you."

"You're a memory?"

"More like a reconstruction. All the memories and feelings and attributions, all rolled into this image."

"But you're a brain mite, Mom. I mean, you were just a minute ago."

"That's where most of me is now. In the bugs. But honey, they aren't what you think. They aren't bad. They're what makes us human."

Robert repositioned himself on the couch, facing her more completely. He looked at the weapon in his hand. He had been told the mites would attack him. And as far as he knew, that's exactly what happened to everyone who went under. But he didn't feel any ill will coming from her. He had no fear, just questions. So many questions. "What do you mean, they make us human?"

She poured herself a drink and lit a cigarette.

"Ok love, here's the deal. I know you are completely obsessed and disgusted by these things. You've demonized them because you needed something to blame, something besides me to see as the cause of all your pain. So, this might take some getting used to, but the brain mites are as much a part of us as our skin. It was when the human race picked up brain mites that we became self-conscious and our neocortex bloomed into its folded spongy magnificence. Without them, we'd still be in caves. And it's all because the brain mites eat the bad stuff. They hold it in their bellies so we can think about other things. Sometimes they get too full and they burst and there's a flood of bad memories. But sweetheart, believe me, life would be far worse without them." She paused and took a drink.

"But Arianne, Charles, they seem fine. Really good even." He felt bad for arguing with his mom, but he needed to know what was going on.

"Yes, they do seem fine. And they are. They keep themselves insulated here. But they can't hide forever. It'd be the same for anyone without the mites. For a while everything would be great, but there'd be nowhere to store the bad things when they come, and they will come. Arianne is already starting to crack. She's rushing you into this and you know it." She took a drag from her cigarette and turned her head to blow the smoke away from him.

"How do I know this isn't a trick? You're a brain mite. You know what I know. You're probably using my memories of my mother against me to save yourself. What would happen if I stabbed you with this?" He brandished his oversized eating utensil.

"A little bit of me would die. I'm so sorry that so many of your memories of me are bad ones. Kill the bugs, and you'd wipe me out." Her face was heart-wrenchingly sad. She stubbed her cigarette out in a little metal ashtray and knocked back the rest of her drink. "Look," she said, her demeanor suddenly serious, "you're going to have to leave soon. The drugs are wearing off. Lie to them. Tell them something ridiculous, like you were at the county fair and all the rednecks turned into wood lice and you chopped them up with a pirate sword you won from a midway booth. They'll buy anything you tell them."

It struck him hard that he'd have to leave her again. "Mom," he said, "I miss you."

"I'm right here. I'll be here when you come back. We'll have a drink together now that you're old enough," she smiled a sad smile, "but now you have to go."

Arianne was there when he opened his eyes. "Welcome back," she said. "Tell me everything."

"I was at some kind of county fair."

31
THE PROTEST

"HEY MAN, I'M LEAVING."

It was a beautiful Saturday morning, and Robert had just run into Johnnie Curseword in the hallway when Johnnie dropped this bomb on him.

"What?"

"Yeah, I'm leaving. Arianne filled me in on Phase Two and the whole long-term plan to spread peace and love and shit. Fuck that. I got what I came here for," he tapped the hole in his head. "I'm not signing up for any of that save the world cult shit. And neither should you. Come on. Let's go."

"I can't."

"Why? Because you still have brain bugs? Everybody has brain bugs. Shit man, according to their test I got double what most people have."

"No, that's not it. There's something I need to take care of first." He wondered, should he tell Johnnie about his mom? Tell him he couldn't leave without seeing her one more time? Johnnie probably would have wanted to break into the dosing cabinet, do the thing right now. Or steal a shitload and leave with it. Better to be vague. "Look, Bet is at my apartment. I'll meet you there in a few days."

"Bet's outside with the protesters. I'm going to go get my shit. But listen man, you take more than a week and I'm coming back for you. Understand?"

Johnnie left him there in the hallway.

Bet's outside with the protesters? This was the first Robert had heard about protesters. And Bet was with them? He went to see for himself.

The library and entryway were full of people. Arianne flitted between them like a giant butterfly, smiling broadly, asking "How can I help you?" Robert made his way to the open front doors. There were maybe a dozen protesters out there, about half as many people as there were inside asking questions and filling out applications. The protesters held signs that said "Arrest Arianne!" and "My Mother was Abducted by Forato House" and "Arianne Forato Lobotomized My Child!"

There was a news van there too. Robert looked around for the crew that came with it and found them off to the side, the cameraman pointing his lens toward the building. The reporter stood in front of the camera, side by side with Bet. They had their backs to Robert.

He took a few steps outside, heading in their direction. Then he stopped, frozen between Bet and his mom, between his future and his past. He was in the cameraman's shot, standing there shifting from one leg to the other, forward and back again. He realized that, on camera, he must have looked like a convert, with his shiny forehead tunnel, his skull nugget on a string around his neck. The cameraman pointed a finger at Robert and adjusted the camera to focus on him. Bet and the reporter both turned to look.

Robert ducked back inside and took off toward his room. He passed Johnnie going the other direction. Johnnie stopped and watched him fly by.

32
THE NEW ROBERT

JUST THAT MORNING, Arianne had been talking to Charles. "What if we're wrong? What if we're messing with things we don't understand?" She was still concerned about her last visit with Shiva.

"Love of my life," he said, "I haven't seen you like this in decades. What's going on?"

"I don't know. First there was the Daniel incident, and then Robert's little girlfriend, and now protesters. Are things falling apart?"

"Come here. Let me hold you. Everything's going to be all right. Nothing has changed, not really. It might not be going perfectly according to the plan, but we're still good. Have you seen the change in Robert? He's walking tall, talking straight. He's becoming exactly the person you said he would."

Arianne snuggled into him, like she used to. Charles made things better.

Later, when the protest started and brought the new recruits with it, Arianne thought how apt the saying was: any publicity *is* good publicity. She couldn't have been more in her element. It took three hours of straight sales pitching, but every person who walked through the door had filled out an application and reserved their spot in the new Project Skylight.

She was exhausted when Robert sat down next to her in the dining hall. Elated, but exhausted.

"I'd like to go under again, soon," he'd said. Not timid, not asking. He was indeed coming into his own, and as proud as she felt, she couldn't acquiesce.

"I'm sorry Robert. It wouldn't be safe."

"Was it safe to rush my trepanation and my first trip? I feel fine. I want to go again."

"I'm saying no Robert. I appreciate your eagerness, but we have to follow protocol. There are a lot of eyes on us now."

The old Robert would have dropped it, but the new Robert pushed on. "With all the publicity and new applicants, I figured the study was moot. I thought we'd be moving on to Phase Two."

"Oh no. If anything, with all this public scrutiny it's even more important for us to toe the line. It's only a few more days until your next session. In the meantime, I'd like you to start attending our planning committees. You're going to play a big part, give Project Skylight a voice, be its face. We need to bring you up to speed."

33
STILL FAKING IT

SHIT. **OK**. **NO**, really, shit. I can't do this. No, I can handle this. Such was Robert's zigzag thinking about his decision to stay and take one more trip to see his mom. Plus, now he was going to be on the planning committee? Man, stick around any organization long enough and you'll end up on a committee.

Arianne had told him the sessions would change him. He'd be less insecure, more sure of himself. So he tried to play it cool, something he'd never in his life succeeded in doing. It wasn't easy. He kept busy. A lot of people mistake busy for confident. He trained in the biofeedback room as much as they'd let him. When he couldn't do that, he read. He tried to be friendly and outgoing with the newcomers.

Robert regretted not talking to Bet when he'd had the chance. The protesters didn't come back, so she didn't either. Maybe they'd done what they meant to. Maybe they could only come on weekends. He'd never been part of anything like that, like this. He had no idea how things worked.

He missed Johnnie. Johnnie knew how to pass the time. It occurred to Robert that if things went really well with Bet, Johnnie might be his father-in-law one day. Then it occurred to him that that was a pretty damn optimistic thought. As far as he knew, he hadn't killed a single neurophage, but even stuck here for three more days, alone and facing a very uncertain future, something was different.

Maybe it was because in the short term he had a goal—go back under, talk to his mom. Maybe it was because he had people he cared about and who cared about him. "If you're not out in a week, I'm coming to get you," Johnnie had said. And he would, too.

Maybe it was the hole in his head.

Whatever it was, he needed it to hold out for three more days.

34
ALL BUSINESS

A RIANNE WAS THE last one to show up for the meeting. That was how she liked it, even if the only other people there were Charles, Doctor David, and Robert. When she hit the room, she was all business.

"It's time. I know we said we were going to wait for the study to be published through traditional means, peer reviewed, and we'll still do that. But I think you'll agree that things have changed. We need to take advantage of the publicity we're getting. In three weeks, once the official study is finished, we need to be ready. Doctor David, we need to move full steam ahead with the new volunteers. And Robert, I want you to head up PR. Can you do that?"

"Sure thing," he said, just like he'd been managing ad campaigns all his life.

"Good, I want you ready to hit every marketing avenue we possibly can. Start writing articles, blog posts, tweets, whatever. Be ready for interviews. See what you can get lined up.

"We're going to need bigger facilities and more staff," she continued. "I'd like to see if we can parlay the current study participants into staff positions while keeping them on for Phase Two. That way all staff will have been trepanned and cleansed of neurophages. We're going to need to scout a new location. I'm thinking Los Angeles first and New York within the year. Plus, we keep this facility in case we need to expand the South Wing."

Robert looked up from the notes he was taking. "Won't everybody be vetted though? And properly trained? Why would we need a psych ward?"

Arianne's demeanor broke from businesslike for just a flash. "It's not a psych ward!" She took a breath. "Look, Robert, it's time to fly. It's time to change the world. I'm envisioning trepanation booths at every festival from Rainbow gatherings to Coachella. Country Thunder even. I would partner with Disney if they'd let me. We should look into that. Write that down. Access to the serum will require courses and oversight. But there may be some people who prefer to pass go without being prepared. In that case, we have to be ready to deal with the fallout."

Arianne could tell that Robert wasn't convinced.

"We're talking about the good of the many here, Robert. I don't need to tell you the other side of that equation."

35
MOM, PART THREE

FINALLY, IT WAS time for Robert to go under again. Finally, he would get to ask all the questions he'd been repeating to himself for the last week, trying to make sure he didn't forget anything. Of course, it didn't go quite as planned.

Once Robert was all strapped in, it was Charles who injected him. Such a strange sight, the tiny hypodermic traveling at him, into him, right above his eyes. There was no pain; the brain doesn't have those sensors. There was just the visual, and then he was out.

Robert was back in his childhood home. The place was packed with giant water bears. Wall-to-wall, no room to move. He was startled, but then they seemed to sense he was there and began to wobble out the front door. As they moved, they revealed his mom sitting in her nest, surrounded by ashtrays and used tissues. He took a seat on the couch as the last of the giant bugs left.

She poured two drinks and lit a cigarette.

"Hello sweetheart. Want a drink? How are you?"

"I'm good, I guess. I'm better now that I'm here." He took the drink she handed to him. "I have a ton of questions for you."

"Oh. Well, I'll do my best, but I'm not really her you know."

"But you're everything I remember, and a lot of that has to be subconscious. So, I figure there are a few things I can learn. Like . . . why did you do it? Why did you leave me?"

"Sweetheart, you know why. I messed up. I was so down that all I could think about was how down I was. And instead of crawling through the pain to the other side, if there was another side, I let myself sink into it. You've been there. You know how hard it can be not to wallow in it." She took a drink, took a drag. "God, I wallowed for years. I didn't take these drugs to get better. I took them to get numb. Maybe I didn't know any better. The drinking sure didn't help." She lifted her glass, tipped it toward him in a mock salute, emptied it in one swallow, and poured herself another.

"But you left me," he said, feeling nine years old again.

"I thought it would be better for you, not coming home to a black hole of need every goddamn day."

"You were wrong."

"And so are you."

"If getting rid of the brain mites isn't the answer, what is?"

"I don't know."

"Well then, why not get rid of the bugs? At least I'd be happy for a little while."

"Because, love, it's giving up. It's giving up who you are. It's giving up your past. It's giving up any chance of a future. All I ever wanted was for you to be happy. But if you do this, you never will be. Not really."

"So what do I do?" He slumped back into the couch.

"I don't know. I never found my answer."

They sat for a minute. Robert was trying to remember what else he wanted to ask, but the time pressure made it hard to think. There was no telling when these sessions would end.

"Look," she said, "when you have a decision to make, do the thing that you know is right. And if you have any question, any doubt about it at all, ask somebody who loves you."

"What about you? I can't ask you if I leave Forato House."

"Sure you can. I'm right here. You can control your dreams, right? So get in a cab and come visit."

"What do I do about Arianne? About her plans and all the people who will want to follow her?"

"I don't know." She lit a fresh cigarette off the butt of the one that was almost to the filter. "There's a lot I don't know. All I do know is you need to get far away from this place."

And that was it. Time was up.

36
Breaking Up is Hard to Do

THAT EVENING, ARIANNE sat in the lounge making herself available for small talk with the new recruits. She was pleased with herself again, very aware of her role as midwife to the next stage in human evolution. The word was out about what she was doing and people were receptive to it, to say the least. The phone had been ringing off the hook, and Arianne's attention was in high demand.

She sat in a high-backed arm chair and held court, smiling and being charming. She was too swept away by the recent series of fortuitous events, too swept away in the rush of the moment, to check her ego. If she'd taken even a moment to consider it, she'd have seen that it was swollen to the size of a zeppelin, and was just as prone to self-destruction.

Robert entered the room with his duffle bag slung over his shoulder. It was rounded out with all of his belongings. He was well into his stride across the lounge when Arianne realized he had no intention of stopping.

"Robert!" she called out.

He stopped and turned toward her. Calmly, he said, "Arianne."

She heaved herself up from the chair, shooing away her recent conversation partners' attempts to help her. Huffing over to Robert, she grabbed him by the elbow and led him to an unoccupied far corner of the room.

"What are you doing?" she asked in an angry whisper.

"I'm leaving," he said. "I'm going home."

"You can't."

"Yes I can, Arianne. What you're doing here, I don't want to be a part of it anymore."

"But," she stammered, "but you *are* a part of it. I saw it. You're going to tell everyone about us. You have to." She took a breath, surprised as how desperate she had suddenly become. She was shaken to her core at the thought of losing Robert. She needed him. He was young and good looking. He had the voice, the demeanor, and a great story. It was just the way of the world—no one would listen to an overweight middle-aged woman in a kaftan.

"This new person you've become," she went on, "I *made* you that way. If it weren't for me you'd still be that sniveling, unsure mouse you were when we first met. You owe me."

"You're right," Robert said. "I owe you my gratitude, and you have it. But I'm not going to kill off my brain mites, so this new me might be temporary anyway. We'll just have to wait and see." He started to move away from her.

"Don't go!" She grabbed his arm.

"Look, I appreciate all you've done for me—I really do—but I'm leaving now."

And he walked away, leaving Arianne looking bewildered and deflated.

37
JOINING THE CARNIVAL

ROBERT HAD NEVER been happier to get to his shithole apartment. He found Bet and Johnnie in the middle of making a late dinner. And while the spaghetti sauce smelled amazing, Robert opted for a peanut butter sandwich, unable to put the sight of a neuron-slurping tardigrade out of his mind.

The three of them ate sitting cross-legged on the floor. Robert and Bet sat close together, his left knee and her right knee touching. Waves of energy emanated from the point of contact and pulsed through him. Johnnie sat across from them, and Theodore, who had nearly doubled in size over the last few weeks, sat in the middle of them all, occasionally lunging at one plate or another and making off with his kill.

"Dude, what the fuck was so important you had to stay?" Johnnie asked Robert.

"My mom," he said. Then he told them all about what he had learned, about brain mites being the repository for humanity's negative memories; about how they let people forget the shit show and get on with living; and about the consequences of getting rid of them—how it would erase whole swaths of a person's past—of who a person was—and how, when things started to go downhill, there wouldn't be any brakes.

"That makes a lot of sense considering what we've seen," Bet said. Then it was her turn to share what she'd learned about the subjects who'd been damaged by the experiments, about the empty stares and lack of personality they shared. She told him about the obsessions that sprouted when bad things happened to them, about the paranoia and the violence toward themselves and others.

Bet put the pieces together. "If there is nowhere to store the bad stuff, it would permanently be at the forefront of consciousness. If you couldn't help but constantly think about every fucked up thing that's happened to you, or that you've heard or seen or read about, of course you're going to flip your lid!"

"So, so, so," Johnnie interjected, "what do you guys want to do about it?"

"Do we need to do anything?" Robert asked. He was happy enough just to be home.

"Fuck yes we do," Johnnie said. "The only reason I'm not a fucking zombie is because I had brain mites to spare."

"And I've already talked with a bunch of people who've been affected. They all want to know what we're going to do next," Bet said. "I'm not going to stop now just because the people I love are safe."

Robert's train of thought derailed. She said she loved him. He kissed her. It was a serious kiss, the kind where feel-good chemicals rush out from your spine and buzz through your body. The kind you never want to end. And while he wouldn't have ever chosen the combination of tomato sauce and peanut butter, in that moment nothing could have been more delicious.

Johnnie Curseword cleared his throat, and the young couple begrudgingly broke apart.

"So, what do we do about Arianne?" Johnnie asked.

"We should sleep on it," Bet said, as Robert gathered up their empty plates. "Dad, why don't you go check out the motel tonight, my treat."

"Sure thing, sure thing," Johnnie said. "I know the score."

Robert was up early the next morning, energized with a sense of purpose—something still new to him. Maybe it was being with Bet. Maybe it was because the effects of the trepanation hadn't worn off yet. Maybe it was knowing that he was in a position to help save an untold number of people from making a life-ruining and potentially life-ending decision. Whatever the cause of his newfound motivation, Robert was going to ride the wave as long as it lasted.

He got straight to work on the PR campaign Arianne had assigned him, except with the opposite message. He spent the morning writing and distributing press releases, and with every email he sent he offered to do an interview or a guest blog, some type of personalized follow-up. He was buried in the process when Johnnie came pogoing in around noon.

"Hey man, whatchya doin, whatchya doin? More online bullshit? You can't do that. Fuck that. That's just what Bet did. You do it that way and you're just going to give Arianne more victims. Listen, listen, what we need to do is we need to go straight to the people. We need to hit the road." And this last part he accentuated with jazz hands, with his whole left hand and his bifurcated right. "We need to join the motherfucking carnival, baby!"

"He's right," Bet added, leaning out of the bathroom door. "I could get you guys jobs with Otis. The carnival always needs rousties."

A ha! Robert thought. Not only do they still use the word, but Robert himself was going to be a roustabout.

✱✱✱

They headed out the next day after leaving Theo with Captain Lou next door. Robert could have been mistaken, but he thought he saw the great big man shed a tear when he took hold of the little fur ball.

Crammed into Bet's old Civic, they drove north for two days to meet up with the carnival. Otis took them on, glad to have the help and to have his fire-eating acrobat back, and they settled in to a whole new kind of life.

Before they would get to a new location, they would set up a time and place for Johnnie to teach piercers how to give safe trepanations. The idea was to spread the knowledge around, making it impossible for Arianne to corner the market.

On the day they rolled into town, they would help set up the midway and the rides, and then head to the shop that was hosting them. Usually there'd be a pretty good turnout. Sometimes local journalists would show up; sometimes reporters would track them down at the carnival.

Robert took the lead in telling their story. He was great at it—charming and humble, charismatic and relatable. He started with his brain bug obsession and failed suicide, and walked them all the way through the murders at Forato House, right up to the test subjects who had been sacrificed to Arianne's cause.

"I was wrong," he would say, "to want to get rid of my brain mites. There are no probiotics for the mind. You can't just eat some yogurt or drink some kombucha and make it all better." (He'd pause here while people chuckled.) "Maybe one day there will be a way to transplant or replenish neurophages, but for now when they're gone, they're gone. And without them, we're fucked."

✳✳✳

Over the months, as they traveled through Idaho and Washington, Oregon and northern California, they watched from afar as Arianne fumbled around. It took a while for her to get any traction. Without her spokesperson, she'd had to come up with a new plan to gain mindshare. She put out a book. She made videos and started a YouTube channel. But most of the press she received was from reporters and bloggers who had heard Robert speak and were trying to appear diligent in getting both sides of the story. In a way, she had been right all along—Robert was telling the world about Project Skylight. It just wasn't happening the way she wanted it to.

Every time they saw her, in the news or in her videos, she looked a little worse for wear, a little more defeated.

38
LOST HER SPARK

"WHAT CAN I do to make you happy, my love?"

Charles had been asking the same question every day for months.

Arianne had started to change the minute Robert walked away. Over the weeks and months, she lost faith in her visions and in her mission. She no longer felt a sense of calling. She had continued on though, going through the motions. She gave interviews, wrote articles and even a book, hired professionals to make her look good online. But every time she put her message out there, about a world with no depression, no anxiety, Robert was right there with a rebuttal. His argument was always the same: what would be left? He said that taking away our bad moods and sad memories didn't leave much to work with. He said that taking them away would take away what makes us human. It would take away the reason we become attached to people. It would take away our need to care about anything, our need to act in the world, to work, to create. He said take away our brain mites and you take away our reason to live.

And once people heard what Robert had to say, and saw the early results of Project Skylight, those poor, suffering martyrs, no one could accept Arianne's position that you have to be willing to give up who you are to become everything you might be.

The change was most apparent in the videos she made; in the early ones she's falsely chipper, and over time her energy and self-confidence ebb, until she's not bothering to hide the bags under her eyes or even smile. Arianne had once again lost her spark.

"What can I do to make you happy, my love?" Charles would ask. She would answer, "I wish I knew."

39
ANOTHER END

THEY WERE ON the road when it happened, staying in a cheap motel along the highway, enjoying hot showers and the prospect of sleeping in a real bed. It was Bet's idea to watch Arianne's latest video.

"This place was wifi. Break out the laptop."

Somewhere along the way, Arianne's videos had become a source of morbid entertainment for the three of them. She had gone beyond the morose and dejected poor-me stage and into full blown paranoia. Robert no longer needed to argue his point; Arianne herself had become living proof of what he claimed. Her fears had nowhere to be contained. She couldn't hide them. Her videos had devolved into rants against all of the people who had abandoned her, which was everyone except for Charles, and diatribes about the world not deserving what she had to offer.

Robert set the laptop on the dresser, and they sat on the bed to watch. Immediately, they knew something was different.

Arianne looked crazy, far beyond her last video, like psych-ward crazy. She wasn't wearing a scarf, and an inflamed red ring was clearly visible around her forehead tunnel. It looked irritated or maybe infected. Her unwashed gray hair was slick to her head, and her skin looked sickly pale compared to her garish kaftan.

"My name is Arianne Forato and I was wrong," is how she started the recording. Parts of it sounded scripted and parts of it sounded like she was flying off the rails. "I thought I could make life worth living not only for myself but for the world. I thought I'd found the way. I had a vision of the future that was beautiful. There was only peace and love and shared prosperity for everyone.

"But there were those who couldn't imagine such a future. People so filled with pain and rage and hatred, so convinced of the necessity of their own misery that they dedicated their lives to making sure this beautiful future never came to be.

"You know who you are, vile rodents. Hateful beasts." They knew she meant them, but Robert knew she meant him more than the others.

"What led them to conspire against me, to turn the world against me, I do not know. What I do know is that I'm done. I'm done with the dream. I'm done with the struggle. I concede. I cannot live this way, haunted every moment by my failures. I give up."

And then in the video she picked up a large syringe. Robert didn't recognize the liquid it held. It was much darker than the serum he had been given. She inserted the needle into her forehead and pressed the plunger down. Within seconds, her eyes lost focus and her jaw went slack.

Robert and Bet looked at each other.

Johnnie whispered, "Holy shit."

The camera did not turn off. After several minutes, there was the sound of a door opening. A man's voice said, "Arianne, what are you doing? Arianne. Arianne?"

Charles came into the shot. "Oh my God, Arianne. Oh my God."

And that is how the video ends.

Robert remembered guessing she'd go out like this, back when he assigned methods of suicide to people out of habit. He wished he'd been wrong.

They passed a somber evening, and sometime during the night, when Bet was sound asleep, Robert left their bed and took the laptop into the bathroom. He sat in the dry tub and watched Arianne's last video again. And then again. He watched it over and over, wondering if she felt the same way he had when he tried to kill himself, wondering if her death was his fault, wondering what would happen to Charles now. After watching it a dozen times, he found he couldn't turn it off. Turning it off would mean he'd have to move on, begin to process it, figure out how to cope with the guilt and come to grips with what Arianne had meant to him. He watched until he fell asleep, just as the sun was starting to rise.

***

Eventually, the high from the trepanation wore off completely. Robert knew it was coming, but he was surprised he didn't crash land. He wasn't ecstatic and in love with the world all the time anymore, but he wasn't completely broken either.

As for him and Bet, they're still together. He goes on hoping that he won't break again, at least not until she leaves him, or dies. And he's pretty sure that if he dies first, it won't break her. Not for long, anyway.

Author's Note

Thanks for reading *Skull Nuggets*. Please don't put a hole in your head because of it.

All of the history of trepanation in here is true, right up to Peter Halvorson's medical tourism studies. But what I didn't include were the stories from people who trepanned themselves, or otherwise acquired a hole in their head, who say it doesn't work. The consensus seems to be that there's a rush that wears off after a couple of weeks or months.

Nor did I mention the arguments from neurologists against the brain blood-volume theory. They point out quite simply that we already have a hole in our skull. It goes down our neck. And removing a tiny portion of the outer skull makes no difference in how much blood the brain can hold or in its pulsation.

So why does trepanation have the reputation it does? How come there are folks who claim it's the best? Probably some mixture of self-fulfilling prophecy, surviving a near-death experience, and finally doing something drastic to change a bad situation. If you find yourself considering trepanation, I'd urge you to read everything you can about it, not just the stuff that supports it.

But Amy, you may be asking, if you don't think it works, why did you spend so much time researching and writing about it? Because it appealed to me as an action rife with symbolism that would make for a nifty storytelling device. So if you're going to drill a hole in your head, please don't pin it on me. But maybe let me know how it goes when you're about six months in.

ABOUT THE AUTHOR

Amy M. Vaughn sits alone in a room with her cats and writes weird little books. This is her idea of a good time.

Boiled Americans by Michael Allen Rose

Boiled Americans is a puzzle box in book form, inspired by the violence of living in urban America and exploding the tendency to forget or ignore.

Great American Slasher by David C. Hayes

Baseball, apple pie . . . and murder.

The Bohemian Guide to Monogamy by Andrew Armacost

Here, a strange labyrinth of interlinked short fiction assembles itself into a darkly moving novella that deftly explores the bottomless pain and pleasure of love and commitment, the hinterland between youth and adulthood.

Surreal Worlds edited by Sean Leonard

An anthology of surrealistic compositions created by some of the finest names in genre fiction. A showcase of international talent undaunted by the conventions of language and common narrative structures. Here is timelessness. Here is Surreal Worlds

How to Succesfully Kidnap Strangers by Max Booth III

Do not respond to bad reviews. If you must respond to bad reviews, please do not kidnap the reviewer.

ADHD Vampire by Matthew Vaughn

He came, he conquered, he was distracted a lot

Notes from the Guts of a Hippo by Grant Wamack

A rugged journalist travels to Brazil in search of a missing hippo researcher and the notes left behind lead to something earth shatteringly revelatory.

All Art is Junk by R. A. Harris

Lana Rivers, a girl with paintbrush hair, is missing and it's up to Lancelot, her cyborg knight, and his bionic conjoined twin, Cilia, to find her before her evil father, a disrespected artist turned mad-scientist, performs a terrible experiment on her.

Cherub by David C. Hayes

Cherub wasn't like the other boys—too slow, too rough—but he didn't deserve what that hospital did to him, and now he will make them pay.

Skinners by Adam Millard

Los Angeles, the City of Angels. At least, that's what the brochure says. What it fails to mention is the earthquakes. Oh, and the flesh-eating creatures lying dormant beneath the concrete, waiting for the chance to surface once again. Their wait is over . . .

The After-Life Story of Pork Knuckles Malone by MP Johnson

What's a farm boy to do when his pet pig becomes an evil, decaying hunk of ham with slime-spewing psychic powers?

A Lightbulb's Lament by Grant Wamack

A gentleman with a lightbulb for head wakes up in a world full of darkness, hooks up with a beautiful ex-prostitute, and an old man who can heal people; he travels down south to find the mysterious Creator.

The Horror Show by Vincenzo Bilof

A poetry novel—a narcoleptic, amnesiac Nobel Prize-winning poet becomes the subject of an experiment to cure madness.

Beyond by Jordan Krall

From Jerusalem to Mars, psychiatry and the unraveling of the universe

Gravity Comics Massacre
by Vincenzo Bilof

An absolutely shitty novella involving comic books, aliens, a serial killer, teenagers in an abandoned town, horror-trope dream sequences, and an ending you're going to hate.

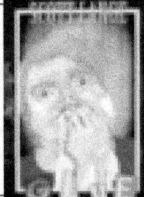

Glue by Scott Lange

Sticky bowels and sticky situations.

Ascent by Matthew Bialer

Is the 8 foot tall creature haunting a small town in Iowa in the fall of the year 1903 the product of a hoax and collective imagination or was it one of the first documented paranormal event in America? This epic poem grapples with these questions.

Elusive Plato by Rhys Hughes

The last in a long decadent line of piratical Spanish eccentrics, Bartleby Cadiz grows up in isolation to be as mad, bad and metaphysical as his ancestors. But he feels there is something different about him. What can it be?

The Fairy Princess of Trains
by Christopher Boyle

Danny's mediocre life turns upside-down when his couch starts whispering to him. Then he's charged with a supernatural mission: Rescue the Fairy Princess of Trains.

Terence, Mephisto & Viscera Eyes
by Chris Kelso

9 new science fiction stories from Chris Kelso

Industrial Carpet Drag by Bruce Taylor

Chemicals make you do great things!

Bizarro Bizarro: An Anthology

The finest bizarro short stories from 2013.

Necrosaurus Rex by Nicolas Day

Necrosaurus Rex tells the tale of Martin, a simple janitor, who takes an unfortunate trip through time, becomes a violent mutant, and the father of us all. There's 14 billion years crushed inside these pages, and most of them are pretty nasty.

Day of the Milkman by S. T. Cartledge

In a world dominated by the milk industry, only one milkman survives after a terrible storm sinks all the ships and throws the Great White Sea out of balance.

Moosejaw Frontier by Chris Kelso

An unapologetic disaster of metafiction

The Boy Who Loved Death by Hal Duncan

From blackest humour to bleakest horror, with twisted relish, Hal Duncan's eighteen tales dig into death—and the life that goes with it.

X's for Eyes by Laird Barron

Between the machinations of the disciples of black gods and good old corporate skullduggery, it's winding up to be of a hell of a summer vacation for the Tooms Brothers.

Omega Grey by Seb Doubinsky

When professor Todd Bailer embarked on a psychedelics quest to discover if the land of the Dead really existed, he had no idea he would threaten the cosmic balance of the universe by triggering a real-estate conquest of the new Frontier.

Berzerkoids by MP Johnson

The first short story collection from Wonderland Book Award-winning author MP Johnson

Retch by David Bernstein

What would you do if you were cursed to puke right before you reached orgasm? You'd do anything, right? (You know you would.) Find out what one wealthy, good-looking, playboy will do to try to end his abhorrent curse.

Static/Orgone by Jamie Grefe

A double-novella of literary grindhouse nightmares and theoretical post-apocalyptic vengeance.

Wonder Weavers by Matthew Bialer

An epic poem about a mysterious sighting in 1896.

Battering the Stem by Bob Freville

A darkly comic urban crime novella. What would it take to make you beg?

Cartoons in the Suicide Forest by Leza Cantoral

When we're dead
You know she'll adore us

www.ingramcontent.com/pod-product-compliance
Lightning Source LLC
Chambersburg PA
CBHW072031170626
46811CB00008B/3034